I'M TRAPPED
IN AN ALIEN'S BODY

HELP!
I'M TRAPPED
IN AN ALIEN'S BODY

TODD STRASSER

AN
APPLE
PAPERBACK

SCHOLASTIC INC.
New York Toronto London Auckland Sydney

To Sophie, Nina, Megan,
and Felix Ryan

ISBN 0-590-76271-0

12 11 10 9   2 3/0

Printed in the U.S.A.   40

First Scholastic printing, March 1998

1

"*Paging Mrs. Ima Hogg.*" The announcement blared out of the science center's loudspeaker. "*Mrs. Hogg, please come to the information desk and meet your son, Ura.*"

Across the lobby from the information desk, my friends Josh Hopka and Andy Kent clamped their hands over their mouths and tried not to laugh out loud.

"Nice going, Jake," they congratulated me as I returned from the information desk, where I'd just asked the information lady to page Mrs. Hogg and her son.

"It's your turn," I said to Andy.

"Ask the information lady to page Ben Dover," Josh urged him.

"Or Amanda Hugginkiss," I suggested.

"I should have known," a voice said behind us.

Andy, Josh, and I wheeled around to find our science teacher, Mr. Dirksen, with his hands on his hips. He gave us a disapproving look.

"Mrs. Ima Hogg and her son, Ura Hogg," Mr. Dirksen chuckled. "When are you boys going to grow up?"

"In about ten years?" Andy guessed.

"More like ten *thousand* in your case," Josh cracked.

"Who said you could leave the rest of the class?" Mr. Dirksen asked.

Without a moment's hesitation, Andy and Josh both pointed at me.

"That's totally bogus!" I sputtered. "It was Andy's idea."

"Was not," Andy denied. "I was led astray."

"Well, you'd better get back to the group," Mr. Dirksen said. "And if you disappear again I'll make sure Principal Blanco hears about it Monday morning."

Mr. Dirksen led us toward the space wing, where the rest of our class was watching a show from NASA. We were on a field trip. It was part of a unit on space.

"I'm particularly disappointed in you, Jake," Mr. Dirksen said as we walked. "First you failed to hand in your report on space, and now I find you paging phony names."

"I hate to say it, Mr. Dirksen," I replied. "But this space stuff just doesn't interest me."

"Does getting an incomplete on your report interest you?" Mr. Dirksen asked.

"Whoa, dudes, check it out!" Andy interrupted us.

I looked around and saw that we had entered a hall lined with all kinds of weird deep-sea fish in glass cases. Most of them had huge eyes, big mouths, and long, sharp teeth.

"Wow, those are some ugly-looking creatures," Josh said.

"Look who's talking," countered Andy. "You're so ugly you have to sneak up on a glass of water."

"Oh, yeah?" Josh shot back. "*You're* so ugly your mother had to feed you with a slingshot."

"That's enough, boys," Mr. Dirksen said sternly. "I don't like those insults, even when they're said in jest. Besides, to you these fish may seem ugly, but they also have a natural beauty. In its own way, nature has designed each one of them perfectly to exist in a hostile environment."

Josh and I shared a doubtful look. "If you say so, Mr. Dirksen."

"Talk about a hostile environment," Andy said as we left the Hall of Fish. "I heard that the temperature is supposed to drop to near zero this weekend."

"Yes, it's going to be unusually cold for this time of year," Mr. Dirksen said. "So if you go outside, you should dress warmly."

"Not on the soccer field," Josh griped. "We've got a practice tomorrow, and then the county championship on Sunday. We're gonna freeze."

"This Sunday?" Mr. Dirksen rubbed his chin. "That's too bad. I'll be out of town at a science conference. Otherwise I'd come watch."

We entered the space wing of the science center and went down a hall lined with oddly shaped hunks of rock.

"Excuse me for asking this, Mr. Dirksen," Josh said, "but why did we have to come all the way to the science center just to watch TV and look at some rocks?"

"These are meteorites, Josh," Mr. Dirksen informed him. "They come from space. Some of them are the famous Mars rocks, which may contain the first real evidence of life on another planet."

"Big space goobers," Andy said.

"What?" said Mr. Dirksen.

"They're shaped like goobers," Andy observed. "Only bigger. Like from really big aliens."

"Yeah." Josh grinned. "You've heard of UFOs? Well, these would be UFGs."

"Unidentified Flying Goobers!" Andy cried.

"Here on display in the Hall of Space Goobers," added Josh.

"You're both being ridiculous," Mr. Dirksen said as he pushed open the door to the lecture room where the rest of our class was. "There are no such things as aliens or UFOs. And there certainly aren't UFGs."

4

"But you just said those Mars rocks showed that there was life on another planet," I reminded him.

"Yes," allowed our teacher. "But it was an extremely primitive form of life. Simple bacteria. Nothing as complicated as an alien."

Inside the lecture room, our class was staring at a TV monitor with rapt attention. Several science center staff members in white jackets were also watching. No one even noticed us come in.

A news reporter was on TV. Behind her was a low white building with a huge satellite dish rising above it.

"This is science editor Rachel Stars, live from the giant Arecibo radio telescope in Puerto Rico," she announced excitedly. "Astronomers here have just confirmed that the strange radio signals detected earlier today were definitely from an unknown source . . . quite possibly an alien lifeform."

A loud gasp went through the lecture room. The science center staff members began a frenzy of whispering. Josh, Andy, and I turned to Mr. Dirksen.

"Didn't you just say there was no such thing as an alien?" Josh asked.

Mr. Dirksen went pale.

2

Meanwhile, on TV, Rachel Stars continued: "No sightings have been confirmed at this time. The only thing astronomers know for certain is that the radio signals came from some kind of intelligent life and did not originate on our planet."

The TV returned to its regular programming. The science center staff members rushed out of the lecture room as if they wanted to get more information. The murmurs and whispers among our class grew louder.

"Do you believe it?" Julia Saks asked. "Intelligent life in outer space!"

"What if it's an attack from Mars!" speculated Alex Silver.

Meanwhile, Josh, Andy, and I were still waiting for Mr. Dirksen to say something. He swallowed, then cleared his throat. "The reporter didn't say the radio waves were *definitely* from aliens. She only said it was possible."

"But the radio waves didn't come from our planet," Andy said. "So they *must* have come from aliens."

Mr. Dirksen shrugged. "We'll just have to wait for more information."

The science center staffers didn't come back to the lecture room, but it was just about time for the field trip to end anyway.

"Okay, everyone," Mr. Dirksen called out. "Let's go back to the bus."

We started back through the space wing and passed the meteorites again.

"Then these really *could* be big space goobers!" Andy exclaimed.

"But they're as hard as rocks," Alex Silver pointed out.

"Maybe they're petrified," Julia Saks suggested.

"That's it!" Andy yelled. "They're big petrified goobers from outer space! From huge aliens with really, really big nostrils!"

The rest of the class laughed. While Andy kept them entertained, Mr. Dirksen took me aside.

"I was wondering if I could ask a favor of you, Jake," he said in a low voice.

"Like what?" I asked.

"I'm going to do a demonstration with my intelligence transfer system tomorrow morning and I'll need some help," he said.

The Dirksen Intelligence Transfer System, or

DITS, was a machine Mr. Dirksen had invented. It was supposed to transfer intelligence from one person to another. But most of the time it just made people switch bodies.

"But tomorrow's Saturday," I said. "Why would I want to come to school on Saturday?"

Mr. Dirksen lowered his voice to a whisper. "Something very exciting has come up. Professor Archibald Orwell from Britain's Royal Academy of Science is coming from England for the science conference on Sunday. But he's going to stop in at school tomorrow to see my invention."

"Sound like an extra-credit project to me," I said with a smile.

Mr. Dirksen thought for a moment. "Suppose I give you an extension on your space report? If you hand it in on Monday, you won't get an incomplete."

"But what am I going to do the report on?" I asked.

"Well, considering today's news," Mr. Dirksen said, "why not do a report on the possibility of life on other planets?"

3

At home that afternoon I was in the den watching a show on our new giant-screen TV when another report came on about those mysterious radio signals. The reporter said that many UFO sightings were being reported, but most were turning out to be fakes, or cases of mistaken identity.

It was starting to sound like the whole alien thing was bogus. I didn't mind because that meant I could do a really short report on the possibility of life on other planets.

My mother and father came into the den. They were both wearing their winter coats.

"So, how do you like our new TV?" Dad asked.

"It's totally awesome, Dad," I said. "Thanks for buying it."

I picked up a bag of Chee-tos and tried to tear it open. It wasn't easy, so finally I put the edge of the bag in my mouth and tore it open with my teeth.

"Hon, I wish you wouldn't watch TV all the time," said my mom.

"Just one more show after this," I said. "Then I promise I'll turn it off."

"Could you stop watching just long enough to say good-bye?" Mom asked.

"Huh?" I looked up from the TV. "Where're you going?"

"We're going to a trade show this weekend," Dad said. "We told you about it, remember?"

I shook my head. I didn't remember them telling me anything.

"We just wanted to say that we're sorry we won't be here Sunday to see you play in the county championship," Mom said.

"Don't sweat it," I said with a shrug. The truth was, I didn't care that much. I was only the backup goalie behind Alex Silver. Most of the time I just stood on the sideline watching Alex play.

In fact, since my parents weren't coming, maybe I'd just skip tomorrow's practice and the championship. It was going to be too cold to play soccer anyway. And this way I could stay home and watch our new TV.

4

At dinnertime I went into the kitchen. My older sister Jessica was there, stirring a big, steaming pot of something yellow with brown and red lumps in it. In the past few years I'd watched her change from your basic annoying good-athlete sister to a super-annoying politically correct dyed-black-hair vegetarian.

Recently she'd changed again. Now she had streaked blonde hair and wore khaki slacks and heavy wool sweaters. She spent most of her time cooking totally gross, disgusting "gourmet" meals, and decorating her bedroom so that it looked like something out of *Snow White and the Seven Dwarfs*.

"Know what's really sad?" Jessica asked as she shook some pepper into the steaming pot.

"That you can't make something simple for dinner," I answered. "Like a cheeseburger."

She glared at me. "That's not what I was going to say. I think it's sad that Mom and Dad had to

11

run off on a business trip. They're going to miss the most important soccer game you'll play this year."

"But they had to go," I said. "It's business."

"Maybe, but it's a shame they can't be here to watch you," Jessica went on. "It's a shame that everything's gotten so complicated and no one has time to appreciate the simple things in life."

"I appreciate the simple things in life," I said. "And that's why I'd really appreciate a cheeseburger for dinner instead of whatever inedible mush you're making."

"For your information, this is not inedible mush," Jessica shot back as she reached for a jar of spice. "It's jambalaya and that's not what I'm talking about. I'm talking about taking time to enjoy life and family. About taking time to appreciate the beauty of nature."

"I'm right with you on that," I agreed. "You should see the nature show I just watched on our new giant-screen TV. I felt like I was right there in the jungle with the monkeys and the hippos."

"Give me a break, Jake," my sister groaned. "You're not experiencing the beauty of nature. You're experiencing sitting on a couch watching TV. The rest of the world could disappear and you wouldn't even notice."

"Would, too," I shot back.

"No, you wouldn't," insisted my sister. "All you

want is your TV and your cheeseburgers. Your life is totally bland, Jake."

"Oh, yeah?" I said. "Well, for your information, spice may be nice, but bland is grand."

Jessica rolled her eyes in disbelief. "You are hopeless."

5

They were still reporting the strange radio waves from space the next morning. But there had not been a single verifiable sighting of a UFO, and the scientists were starting to wonder if they'd made a mistake.

That was all I needed to hear. I took out my notebook, sat down at the desk in the den, and did my report:

REPORT ON THE POSSIBILITY OF
LIFE ON OTHER PLANETS
by Jake Sherman

After careful consideration, I have decided that there is no possibility of life on other planets.

THE END

Meanwhile, the temperature outside had dropped to frigid. Sitting in the den, I glanced

14

out the window and saw people bundled up in coats and hats and scarves. I really didn't want to go out. I wished I hadn't promised Mr. Dirksen that I'd help him with the dumb DITS machine at school.

I watched TV for a while. Finally, when I couldn't put it off any longer, I pulled on my warm ski parka and a hat and scarf and left the house.

Brrrrr . . . the air was icy. It wasn't just freezing out, it was windy, too. Waves of yellow and orange leaves swirled around the street, and the wind stung the parts of my face that weren't covered by the scarf and hat.

"Yo, Jake!" someone called from behind me. I turned and saw Andy, Josh, and Alex Silver. They were wearing their soccer cleats, and were bundled up in sweats and team jackets and knit hats. Andy was wearing a blue scarf around his neck and mouth.

"Can you believe we have to practice today?" Andy asked through chattering teeth.

"At least you guys get to run around," Alex said as we walked toward school. "All I do is stand in the goal. That's *really* cold."

Josh gave me a funny look. "Where are your sweats and cleats, Jake?"

"I'm not going to practice," I answered.

The others looked surprised.

"Why not?" Andy asked.

"It's too cold," I said.

"But we have to get ready for the championship tomorrow," Alex said.

"If it's this cold, I'm not gonna play tomorrow, either," I said.

"But you're our backup goalie," Josh said.

"Goalies never get hurt," I replied. "And they don't get tired, either. Alex can play the whole game, no sweat."

My friends shared shocked looks.

"Then why are you going to school?" Andy asked.

"Dirksen asked me to help him with something," I said.

We walked along in silence for a while. I guess my friends didn't know what to say.

"Look, guys, it's not a big deal," I told them. "Alex will play great. You guys won't even miss me."

"That's not the point," Josh argued. "You're part of the team, even if you don't play that much. It won't be the same if you're not there."

My friends tried to convince me to play the next day. Finally I said I'd think about it. We got to school and my friends jogged off toward the soccer field. I was glad to go inside and get out of the cold.

I went down to Mr. Dirksen's lab and knocked on the door.

Mr. Dirksen let me in with a smile. "Glad you could make it, Jake."

I stepped into the science lab. The DITS was across the room near the windows. It was a big computer console with chairs on either side of it and a lot of wires running in between them.

But what caught my attention was the guy standing near the DITS, gazing out the window. He had to be the strangest-looking dude I'd ever seen.

6

Mr. Dirksen led me over to the man. He was shorter than me and wearing a long black coat that dragged on the floor. His face and head were covered by a dark hat, sunglasses, and some kind of white gauze.

"Professor Orwell," Mr. Dirksen said, "I'd like you to meet Jake Sherman, one of my favorite students."

Professor Orwell turned from the window and nodded at me. I thought he'd offer to shake hands, but he kept his hands in the pockets of his coat.

"The professor is an expert on methods of learning," Mr. Dirksen explained. "He wants to see how the Dirksen Intelligence Transfer System works."

Meanwhile, Professor Orwell didn't say a thing. The more I looked at him, the more I was convinced that he was one weird guy.

"So what do you need me for?" I asked.

Mr. Dirksen looked surprised. "I thought it would be obvious, Jake. I'm going to use the DITS to download Professor Orwell's knowledge into my own mind. At the same time, the professor will receive everything I know. What better way to demonstrate my invention."

I stared at my teacher in disbelief. He couldn't be serious. "Uh, do you think we could have a word in private, Mr. Dirksen?"

"Of course, Jake." Mr. Dirksen turned to our visitor. "Please excuse us, Professor. Jake and I have to discuss some details. We'll be right back."

Professor Orwell nodded silently and looked out the window again. Mr. Dirksen and I went out into the hall.

"What's the problem, Jake?" my teacher asked.

"What makes you think the DITS is going to work?" I asked. "I mean, it never works right. All it ever does is make people switch bodies."

"I've fixed that," Mr. Dirksen assured me. "This time the DITS will work exactly the way it's supposed to."

"That's what you said last time," I reminded him.

"I promise you, Jake," Mr. Dirksen said. "Nothing is going to go wrong. Besides, you don't have to worry. You're not receiving Professor Orwell's intelligence. I am."

He had a point, but I was still bothered by

something. "I'm not so sure about this Professor Orwell dude, either."

"Why not?" Mr. Dirksen asked.

"Haven't you noticed that he's wearing a disguise?" I asked.

"Oh, no, Jake, you've got it all wrong." Mr. Dirksen chuckled. "He was in a terrible accident a few weeks ago. His face and hands were burned."

"Why doesn't he talk?" I asked.

"It's painful for him," Mr. Dirksen said. "He has a speech problem. That's why it's so important that we use the DITS. It's the only way anyone else can learn everything he knows. Now let's go back in before he becomes impatient."

7

Inside the lab, Professor Orwell had left his place beside the window. Now he was standing near a display case, holding a bright yellow-and-orange leaf some kid must've brought into school. He was staring at it so intently that you would have thought he'd never seen a leaf before.

"Professor Orwell, would you mind stepping over to the DITS and sitting down?" Mr. Dirksen asked.

The professor started toward us. He walked slowly and had to stop halfway across the room to catch his breath. I gave Mr. Dirksen a puzzled look.

"He's still recovering from the accident," my teacher whispered.

Finally the professor came over and sat in one of the chairs. Mr. Dirksen sat in the other chair. I stepped behind the computer console.

"I've already made the proper adjustments, Jake," Mr. Dirksen said. "All you have to do is push the red button."

I looked down at the computer console and saw the red button. But I also noticed that the needle on the brain density meter was deep in the red.

"One of these meters is in the danger zone," I said.

Mr. Dirksen frowned. "That's not possible." He got up from his seat and joined me at the console. "Hmmm, you're right. I'm sure it's just an electrical short. Jake, would you mind sitting in my chair so I can run a test?"

I went over and sat in the chair Mr. Dirksen had been sitting in. On the other side of the computer console, Professor Orwell sat perfectly still and didn't say a word.

Frankly, I thought the guy was totally bizarre.

Mr. Dirksen turned some dials on the computer console. "Very odd," he mumbled to himself. "The brain density meter seems to be operating properly, but the reading it's giving for the professor isn't humanly possible."

Thwunk! The door to the science lab suddenly flew open and Josh and Andy charged in.

"Jake!" Andy called to me. "You won't believe what happened!"

"Huh?" Mr. Dirksen spun around.

The last thing I saw was his elbow hitting the red button.

Whump!

Everything went black.

8

I couldn't believe it.

Mr. Dirksen had sworn he'd fixed the DITS.

He *promised*!

But as soon as I heard that *whump!* I knew exactly what had happened.

I'd switched bodies with Mr. Weirdo Professor!

The haze cleared. I was sitting in the seat on the other side of the computer console, in Professor Orwell's body.

Mr. Dirksen, Andy, and Josh were staring at us with surprised expressions.

"Professor Orwell, Jake . . . are you all right?" Mr. Dirksen gasped.

"Who's that guy?" Andy pointed at me in Professor Orwell's body.

Before Mr. Dirksen could answer, Professor Orwell, who now had my body, stood up and looked down at himself. What he saw was my body, arms, and legs. He held up one of my hands and wiggled my fingers. Then he looked down at my legs and shook them. A big smile appeared on his — I mean, my — face.

The next thing I knew, Professor Orwell, in my body, dashed across the lab, yanked open the door, and disappeared.

"Wait, Jake!" Josh ran to the door and yelled after him. "Come back!"

Josh stood in the doorway for a second, then came back into the lab. "He took off down the hall and ran outside."

"I guess that loud *whump* must have startled him," Mr. Dirksen mused. "Still, it's not like Jake to run away."

I probably should have informed them that the person they thought was me wasn't Jake at all, but Professor Orwell with my body.

Only, I was distracted by the body I was now inhabiting.

I'd been stuck in some pretty strange bodies before.

Like my dog's.

And my gym teacher's.

And even the body of the President of the United States.

But I'd never been stuck in a body like this.

In fact, I wasn't sure you could call it a *body*.

9

Inside the long black coat, Professor Orwell's arms felt really constricted. So I took his hands out of his pockets. He was wearing gray wool mittens. It was dumb to wear mittens inside, so I pulled them off. But the hands underneath weren't hands! They were like the mittens I'd just taken off. Each hand had one flat flipperlike thing and a long skinny thumb opposite it.

Boy, that Professor Orwell really did have one weird body!

Across the room, Josh, Andy, and Mr. Dirksen all reacted the same way when they saw my hands. Their mouths fell open.

Next I pulled off the hat and unwound the bandages from around my — I mean, Professor Orwell's — face.

As the bandages fell away from my face, Mr. Dirksen, Josh, and Andy all stepped back and stared at me in horror.

"Yuck!" Andy wrinkled his nose in disgust.

"Gross!" Josh stuck out his tongue.

"Most unusual," Mr. Dirksen muttered in wonder.

I reached up and touched my eyes with my mitten-hand. My eyes felt huge, as if they were the size of tennis balls!

I moved my mitten-hand down to where my nose should have been.

But I didn't have a nose! Just two stubby tubes with holes at the ends.

Moving my mitten-hand down farther I came to the place where a mouth should have been. I could feel an opening, but it was hard . . . like a beak or something.

Meanwhile, Mr. Dirksen, Josh, and Andy backed slowly toward the door, as if they were afraid that I was going to do something terrible to them.

"Where are you going?" I asked, but my voice came out in a high-pitched squeak.

Across the room, Mr. Dirksen and my friends stopped and looked surprised.

"You can talk?" Mr. Dirksen asked.

"Of course I can," I squeaked. "Why shouldn't I?"

"Because you're . . ." Mr. Dirksen's voice trailed off.

"I'm what?" I squeaked.

Mr. Dirksen, Josh, and Andy shared a nervous look.

"You're . . . not from this world," my teacher said.

"I am, too," I squeaked.

"No, you're not," said Josh.

"Yes, I *am*," I insisted. "Why can't I be?"

Andy took a deep breath as if he were mustering his courage. "Well, sir, to be perfectly blunt, you can't be from this planet because we don't have *anything* as ugly as you."

"Very funny, dimwit," I shot back.

Mr. Dirksen and my friends shared another look.

"Did he just call you a dimwit?" Mr. Dirksen asked Andy.

Andy nodded.

"Is it possible that aliens use that expression, too?" Mr. Dirksen asked.

"I think I'd know if I was an alien," I squeaked. "I know this body may be weird, Mr. Dirksen, but even you said there's no such thing as an alien."

Mr. Dirksen swallowed nervously. "I think I just changed my mind."

10

"**W**ait a minute." Josh took a step closer and peered suspiciously at me. "Who are you?"

"I'm Jake," I squeaked. "Who do you think I am?"

Mr. Dirksen blinked. "You're Jake?"

"That's right, Mr. Dirksen," I squeaked. "Know what that means?"

"The DITS is still malfunctioning!" Mr. Dirksen realized.

"You got it," I squeaked bitterly.

"You're really Jake?" Andy asked as if he still couldn't believe it.

"That's right." I pointed my mitten-hand at Mr. Dirksen. "And you *promised* this wouldn't happen again!"

Mr. Dirksen looked stunned. He pointed at the lab door. "Then the person who has your body is an alien, not Professor Orwell."

Meanwhile, Andy whispered something in Josh's ear, and they both began to grin.

Then their grins became smiles.

And their smiles became chuckles.

"Would someone like to tell me what's so funny?" I squeaked.

But my friends were now laughing too hard to answer.

"All I did was switch bodies with an alien," I squeaked.

Andy shook his head. His face was red and it looked like he was having trouble breathing. "No, that's not *all* you did. You not only switched bodies with an alien, Jake. You switched bodies with . . . a *funny-looking* alien!"

11

Josh and Andy were doubled over, laughing.
"This isn't funny, guys," I squeaked.

"You're right!" Josh cried. "It's hysterical!"

I gave Mr. Dirksen a pleading look. He was a grown-up. He had to be more mature about this than my friends.

"Ahem." He cleared his throat. "I don't think you boys understand the incredible importance of this moment. Don't you realize that we are the first humans to ever have contact with an alien being?"

"Even if he is the funniest-looking alien since Yoda from the *Star Wars* movies," Andy added.

Mr. Dirksen pressed his lips together tightly. It seemed like he was fighting the desire to smile. "I do not approve of your use of the phrase *funny-looking*. I find it personally offensive."

"Oh, yeah?" Josh guffawed. "Then what phrase would you use?"

Mr. Dirksen bit his lip and looked at me. "Well,

er, I hate to say this, Jake, but as an example of extraterrestrial life . . . you are somewhat amusing-looking."

"Amusing-looking!" Josh cackled.

That was it! I had to see my new face. I looked around the lab for a mirror. At first I didn't see any, but then I noticed the shelf where the microscopes were stored. They all had little mirrors under them!

I tried to hurry over to the microscopes.

Only, I couldn't go very fast. My stubby little alien legs moved slowly and got tired almost immediately. After only a few steps, I was breathing hard and had to stop and rest.

Josh and Andy were still doubled over in laughter. Even Mr. Dirksen was smiling.

I tried walking again and was soon gasping for breath. But finally I made it over to the microscopes. I was sort of worried that I wouldn't be able to see myself very clearly in the tiny mirror.

But amazingly, I could see myself perfectly. It must have been those big eyes.

"Ahhhhhhhhhhhhhhhhhhhhhhhhhhhhh!" A high-pitched scream left my beaklike mouth.

They were right!

I was the funniest-looking alien I'd ever seen!

12

If you've seen the *Alien* movies, or *Predator*, then you know that some aliens can look pretty mean and ugly.

And usually, the uglier they are, the *scarier* they are.

I sure was ugly enough with those big, bulging eyes that made me look like a frog.

And skin so pale you could see the veins and muscles underneath.

And those two stubby tubes for a nose.

And that beak thing for a mouth.

Not to mention two big floppy ears sticking out sideways that made me look like one of those spitting dinosaurs from *Jurassic Park*.

Except compared to me, those spitting dinosaurs looked great.

I was *that* ugly.

But for some strange reason, I wasn't scary.

And when you're an ugly alien, but not a *scary* alien . . .

Then you're a funny-looking alien.

"I gotta stop laughing or I'm gonna barf!" Josh grunted.

"Go ahead," Andy cried. "Even barf would look better than Jake!"

"That's a terrible thing to say, Andy," Josh guffawed.

I was just about to thank him for coming to my defense when he added, "But unfortunately, it's true!"

"This really isn't funny," I squeaked in my alien voice.

"Listen to that voice!" Josh was laughing so hard he was crying. "He sounds like Mickey Mouse on helium!"

"No." Andy shook his head. "He sounds worse!"

They kept laughing. Andy was doubled over. Josh was holding his sides as if he'd been laughing so hard it hurt. Even Mr. Dirksen had pulled off his glasses and was wiping tears from his eyes.

That was the last straw. I didn't have to stay there and take their abuse. What I had to do was find the alien who had my body and get it back. I started across the lab to get the alien's coat, hat, and sunglasses.

I got about halfway across the room on those stubby little legs. Then I had to stop and rest.

This is ridiculous! I thought as I caught my breath. My legs felt so tired, you would have thought that alien had never walked anywhere in his life!

Meanwhile, my friends were still laughing. They were really getting on my nerves! I just wanted to put on that coat and get out of there.

I took a few more steps, but had to stop again and rest. At this rate it was going to take forever just to get across the room.

Then I remembered that my alien arms were pretty long. Maybe, if I really stretched them, I could reach the coat.

I stretched my arms out.

They stretched . . .

And stretched . . .

And stretched!

The next thing I knew, I had the coat, hat, and sunglasses in my mitten-hands.

Josh and Andy stopped laughing.

"Did you see that?" Josh asked.

"His arms stretched nearly six feet," Mr. Dirksen exclaimed in amazement.

13

"That's not possible," Andy said.

"It is if he's an alien," Josh reminded him.

Alien, schmalien. I was getting out of there. I pulled on the coat, hat, and sunglasses.

"Wait!" Mr. Dirksen cried. "Where are you going?"

"I'm going to find that alien and get my body back," I squeaked.

"Can't say I blame you," Andy said with a grin.

"How about you guys coming with me and helping me find him?" I squeaked.

Andy and Josh shared a look.

"Would you want to go anywhere with someone who looked like that?" Andy asked.

Josh shook his head.

"Come on, guys," I pleaded. "I thought you were my friends."

Andy sighed reluctantly. "Coach Roberts did tell us to go find Jake. That was why we came in here in the first place."

"What are you talking about?" I squeaked.

"Alex twisted his ankle in practice," Andy explained. "He won't be able to play in the championship tomorrow. Coach Roberts wanted us to get you because you're the backup goalie."

"He *was* the backup goalie," Josh corrected him. "Then he had to go and switch bodies."

"It's not my fault!" I squeaked. "*You're* the ones who barged in here and made Mr. Dirksen push the dumb button."

"Right, Jake," Josh scoffed. "Blame it on us."

"Stop it!" Mr. Dirksen shouted. "Don't you boys understand what's going on here? We are dealing with *an alien*! Nothing like this has ever happened before! This is a major historical event! When the world learns —"

"— that it's just Jake in an alien's body, the world is *not* going to be impressed," Andy finished the sentence for him. "In fact, I think they're gonna be pretty ticked at you for taking the first alien to ever visit Earth and mixing him up with an everyday kid."

"That's probably like alien abuse or something," Josh added.

Mr. Dirksen's shoulders sagged. "Well, I admit it's not as impressive as if it were an alien in an alien's body."

"So let's find him and switch me back," I squeaked.

"Yeah, it'll be like getting two birds with one

stone," Josh said. "We'll get the alien back in the alien's body so Mr. Dirksen can impress the world. And we'll get Jake back in Jake's body so that he can play goalie tomorrow."

I reached for the door with my mitten-hand and pulled it open. Outside stood a tall man with white hair. He was wearing a gray coat and carrying a suitcase.

"Excuse me," he said. "I'm here to see Mr. Dirksen."

14

The tall man with the white hair turned out to be the *real* Professor Orwell. It was a good thing I'd put on the alien's disguise or he might have freaked when he saw me.

Even worse, he might have laughed.

Mr. Dirksen greeted Professor Orwell and asked him if he'd mind waiting in the lab for a little while. For the next hour Mr. Dirksen was nice enough to drive us around in his car. We tried all the logical places where a visitor from another planet might want to go — the mall, the video arcade, and McDonald's. But there was no sign of him.

"I have to admit that this is a very strange experience," Mr. Dirksen said as he drove. "Here we are looking for Jake Sherman, and yet he's in the car with us."

"We're just looking for my body," I reminded him from the backseat, where I was bundled up in the coat, hat, and sunglasses.

Andy looked over the front seat at me. "I hate to say this, Jake, but I can see why that alien was eager to get out of his body and into yours. I still can't get over how *funny-looking* you are."

"And you can't seem to stop reminding me, either," I sulked.

"In the alien's defense," Mr. Dirksen said, "I would like to point out that while the body Jake is currently inhabiting is rather . . . unusual, it may be perfectly suited for the world he comes from."

"Then that alien dude must come from a really, *really* funny-looking world," Josh observed.

"Know what, guys?" I squeaked. "I'd be really, *really* happy if I didn't have to hear the phrase *funny-looking* again."

"Jake is right," Mr. Dirksen said. "There has to be another way to describe his appearance."

"How about repulsive?" Andy suggested.

"Or disgusting?" asked Josh.

"No, no," said Mr. Dirksen. "Something not so negative. Let's agree that from now on we'll just say that Jake is . . . er, *interesting.*"

"Oh, yeah." Josh smirked.

"Can I just tell one funny-looking joke?" Andy begged me.

"Remember, Andy, we're going to use the word *interesting* from now on," Mr. Dirksen reminded him.

"Okay," Andy agreed. "One *interesting* joke?"

"Go ahead." I gave in. "But promise it'll be just one."

"I promise," Andy said. "Okay, here goes: You're so *interesting* you give Freddy Krueger nightmares."

"I've got one!" Josh chimed in. "Jake's so *interesting* his reflection got scared and ran away."

"That's nothing," Andy said. "Jake's so *interesting* he walked into a haunted house and came out with a job."

"How about this one?" Mr. Dirksen said. "Jake's so *interesting* he gives aspirin a headache!"

"Here's a better one," said Andy. "Jake went to an *interesting* contest and the judges said, 'Sorry, no professionals.'"

"How about, he's so *interesting* he has to trick-or-treat by phone?" Mr. Dirksen asked.

"Good one!" Josh yelled.

The next thing I knew Josh, Andy, and Mr. Dirksen were congratulating one another and exchanging high fives.

"I thought you said you were only going to tell one joke," I grumbled.

Everyone grinned sheepishly.

"I guess we got carried away," Andy said.

Mr. Dirksen looked at his watch. "I have to get back to the lab, boys. Professor Orwell is waiting.

He and I have to leave for the science conference."

"You can't!" I squeaked. "Without a car, how are we going to look for the alien who took my body?"

"I'm not sure having a car matters," Mr. Dirksen replied. "We have no idea where to look for him, Jake."

"But we have to keep trying," I squeaked.

Mr. Dirksen said he was really sorry, but he couldn't make the real Professor Orwell wait any longer. He promised that he'd call the next night when he got back from the conference. If we'd found the alien who had my body by then, he'd meet us at school early Monday morning to help us switch back.

Josh, Andy, and I spent the rest of the day searching for the alien by ourselves. My friends found an old shopping cart and pushed me around in it. But we couldn't find the alien who had my body.

"I've had it," Andy finally complained. "I'm freezing and tired and cold. Besides, it's getting dark."

"He's right," Josh agreed. "In another fifteen minutes it'll be too dark to pick anyone out of a crowd."

I slumped down miserably in the shopping cart. "What if I'm stuck in this body forever? What am I going to do?"

"You could join the circus," Andy suggested.

"That Amazing *Interesting* Jake, Half Alien, Half Human," Josh added.

"Thanks, guys," I groaned woefully. "I really appreciate your support."

15

A few minutes later my friends stopped on the sidewalk outside my house and helped me out of the shopping cart. Now that it was dark out, it was even colder. We were all shivering.

Josh scuffed his foot against the curb. "Well, Jake, I guess I'd better get going." His breath came out in a white plume of vapor.

"Me, too," Andy said, bouncing up and down on his toes to stay warm.

"You're just going to leave me here?" I squeaked miserably.

"What else can we do?" Andy asked.

I didn't have an answer. I just hated being stuck in that body.

"Look, Jake, don't worry," Josh said. "You'll probably find the alien tomorrow."

"Aren't you going to help me look for him?" I asked.

Josh and Andy shared a glance.

"We'd like to, but we've got the soccer championship," Josh said.

"But I can hardly walk in this body," I squeaked desperately. "I'll never be able to find him alone."

"Ask Jessica to help," Josh suggested.

Jessica . . .

That's when I realized I had another problem. I looked up at my house. Inside, the lights were on.

"How am I going to explain this to my sister?" I asked my friends. "How am I going to prove that it's really her brother inside this yucky alien body? She'll take one look at me and call the cops."

"Don't worry," Andy said. "They'll never arrest you."

"Why not?" I asked.

Andy grinned. "They'll be laughing too hard."

"No, no." Josh nudged Andy with his elbow. "They won't arrest him because if they put him in jail the other prisoners would try to escape!"

"Or, how about— " Andy started to say.

"Shut up!" I screamed.

16

I had to beg Josh and Andy to come in and help explain to Jessica who I was so that she didn't freak out when she saw me. We went up to the front door. I didn't have my key. It was in my clothes, which the alien was now wearing. I was just about to knock when Josh stopped me.

"What's wrong?" I asked.

"I think I'd better knock," he said.

"Why?" I asked.

"Because if she sees you first she may slam the door in your face," Andy said. "Take my scarf and wrap it around your head."

Andy gave me his scarf. Then he and Josh got in front of me and knocked on the door.

"Who is it?" Jessica called from inside.

"Josh and Andy," Josh answered.

The door opened. Peeking between my two friends, I could see my sister. But she didn't notice me.

"Hey, guys, what's up?" Jessica asked.

"Well, uh, I'll bet you're wondering where Jake is," Josh said.

"Not really," Jessica admitted. "But now that you mention it, why isn't he with you?"

"He is," Andy said.

Jessica frowned and looked around. "Where?"

"Here." Josh and Andy parted so that she could see me in the shadows behind them.

My sister looked down at me in the alien's body and blinked. "That's not Jake."

"Yes, it is," Andy said.

"No way," said Jessica. "Jake's not a shrimp. He's as tall as you are, Andy." She looked back down at me. "Who are you, anyway? Why are you wearing sunglasses at night?"

I didn't want to answer her. I didn't want her to hear that squeaky alien voice.

"It's Jake," Josh said. "I swear, Jessica. We were in Dirksen's lab. The DITS went on by accident."

Jessica stared at Josh. The blood drained from her face as she realized what must have happened. She knew all about the DITS.

"Ohmygod!" She grabbed Josh and Andy by their collars. *"What did you do to my brother?"*

17

"We didn't do anything to him," Josh wheezed as he tried to pull my sister's hand off his collar.

"It was all Mr. Dirksen's fault," Andy added.

Jessica couldn't take her eyes off me. Luckily, with the hat, sunglasses, and Andy's scarf wrapped around my face, she couldn't see what I really looked like.

"Let's go inside." She shivered. "It's freezing."

We all went into the house. My sister closed the door and bent down to face me. "Who did you switch with, Jake?"

I remained silent.

Jessica looked up at Josh and Andy. "Why won't he talk?"

"It's really bad this time," Josh warned her.

Jessica looked puzzled. "Worse than switching with our dog, Lance?"

"Way worse," said Andy.

My sister's eyes widened. She stared warily at

me. "Worse than switching with . . . a monkey?"

"Oh, yeah." Josh nodded.

Just then I heard the pad of paws on the floor as Lance came down the hall. He stopped in front of me and started to sniff. I braced myself. Lance didn't like strangers. He'd been known to attack if he felt threatened.

Lanced stopped sniffing.

Then he turned sideways . . .

And started to lift his leg!

18

"**L**ance, stop!" Jessica yelled. She grabbed him by the collar and yanked him away. "I've never seen Lance do that before."

Josh and Andy shared another look.

"And yet, somehow I'm not surprised," Andy quipped.

"Why?" Jessica asked. "How bad could it be?"

"Worse than you can imagine," Josh cautioned her. "Like something from another planet."

"Another planet?" my sister sputtered. "That's ridiculous. There's no such thing."

"Where have I heard that before?" Andy asked with a grin.

Jessica turned to me again. "Jake, why won't you let me see what you look like? Why won't you talk?"

"I'm warning you," Josh said. "He's in an alien's body."

"There are no such things as aliens," Jessica

stated firmly. "I don't know who this is, but if he won't talk or let me see him, I'm not sure I want him in my house."

It looked like I didn't have a choice. I started to unwrap the scarf. Then I took off the sunglasses and hat.

Jessica's jaw dropped.

"Ahhhh!" She yelped and jumped back. "That's not Jake. It can't be! It's not even human!"

"Maybe not, but it's Jake," Josh said.

Jessica shook her head. "You're playing a trick on me."

"Talk to her, Jake," Andy said to me.

"It's me," I squeaked.

Jessica looked less scared and more puzzled. "What's with the voice?"

"That's the way this alien sounds," Josh said.

Jessica shook her head. "No, I don't believe this. There're no such things as aliens, and that's not Jake."

"I think you'd better prove it to her," Andy suggested.

"It would be nice if you'd make me a cheese-burger," I squeaked. "Than I could enjoy some of the simple things in life."

My sister blinked.

Her eyes widened. "It's really you?"

"Yeah," I squeaked. "And I'll bet you're thrilled."

A smile started to appear on Jessica's face. "I guess there really are aliens after all."

The smile grew larger.

I felt my alien face grow hot. Even my very own sister thought I was funny-looking.

"Oh, wow, Jake," Jessica chuckled. "You've really done it to yourself this time! Just wait till Mom and Dad see you!"

"They won't think it's funny," I squeaked.

"You're right!" Jessica laughed. "They'll think it's *hysterical!*"

Laughter must be infectious, because Josh and Andy were starting to grin again. I couldn't believe it! It was as if nobody cared. Nobody wanted to take this seriously. I was going to be stuck in this yucky, funny-looking alien body for the rest of my life, and they all thought it was a joke!

I could feel my big froggy eyes start to grow watery.

Froggy tears began to roll down my alien cheeks.

Josh was the first to notice. He stopped grinning.

"Hey, what's wrong, Jake?" he asked.

Now Andy stopped smiling and Jessica stopped laughing.

"Aw, we didn't mean to make you cry," Andy said.

"Can't you take a joke, Jake?" Jessica asked.

"It's no joke to me." I sniffed. "I'm the one who's stuck in this crummy excuse for a body. I'm the one who's going to go through the rest of my life with people laughing at me."

Josh, Andy, and Jessica shared a somber look.

"I told him he could be a star if he joined the circus," Andy said.

"I don't want to join a circus," I squeaked, wiping the tears away with my mitten-hands. "I just want my old body back. And you're the only ones I know who can help me."

"How?" Jessica asked.

"By helping me find the alien who has my body and getting it back," I squeaked and sniffed.

Jessica pursed her lips as if she had to think about it. "Okay, Jake. As much as I love the idea of keeping you in this body forever, I promise I'll help you look for him."

I gave Josh and Andy a pleading look.

"But we've got the game tomorrow," Andy said.

"After the game," I squeaked. My alien face was wet with tears and my nose holes were stuffed up. My mom kept a box of tissues on a shelf under the front hall mirror. It was six or seven feet away. I stretched my alien arm and just managed to reach it.

Jessica and the others watched in silent amazement.

"How did you do that?" Jessica asked.

"I don't know," I squeaked. "It's just something this alien body can do."

"Where did this alien come from?" she asked.

"Outer space, I guess. Then he just showed up at school."

Meanwhile, Josh and Andy were whispering heatedly to each other.

"What's with you guys?" I squeaked.

Josh cleared his throat. "Uh, Andy and I were just wondering, Jake . . . You know how Alex twisted his ankle and can't play goalie in the county championship tomorrow?"

"What about it?"

"Josh and I couldn't help noticing that you can stretch those alien arms pretty far," Andy said.

"Which means you'd probably be pretty good playing goalie," Josh added.

"Maybe even better than when you were in your old body," said Andy.

I stared at them in disbelief. "You want me to *stay* in this body so I can play goalie tomorrow?"

"It *is* the championship," Josh reminded me.

"The rest of the team would really appreciate it," said Andy.

"If they didn't die laughing first," I squeaked bitterly and shook my alien head. "No way. Forget it. I'm not playing goalie."

"Aw, come on," Andy said. "Where's your team spirit?"

"In my other body," I snapped. "And that's what I'm going to spend tomorrow looking for. If you guys were truly my friends, you'd help me."

Andy's shoulders slumped. "You *sure* you won't play goalie?"

"Put yourself in my position, Andy," I squeaked. "Would *you* want to play goalie if you were in this body?"

"Come on, Andy." Josh pulled him toward the door. "Let's leave Jake alone. He's got enough problems without having to worry about the soccer team. Even though it *is* the first championship we've ever been in."

"You're just trying to make me feel bad," I squeaked as I followed them to the door. "I wish you were the ones who were stuck in this body. Then you'd understand how I feel."

Josh and Andy stopped at the front door and zipped up their team jackets.

"We're just asking you to think about it, Jake," Josh said. "Mr. Dirksen will be away tomorrow. It's not like you'll be able to switch back into your old body before Monday morning anyway."

"But I don't even know where my body is," I squeaked as Josh reached for the doorknob. "For all I know that alien has already taken my body and gone back to his old planet."

Josh opened the door to leave.

Someone was standing outside the front door.

Since I was standing behind Josh and Andy, he couldn't see me.

But I could see him.

He looked really familiar.

In fact, he looked just like me.

19

"**E**xcuse me. Good evening," the alien who had my body said to Josh and Andy. Thick white vapor escaped his lips as he spoke. His teeth were chattering from the cold and he was hugging himself to stay warm. "I'm terribly sorry to disturb you, but is this the residence of Jake Sherman?"

Josh and Andy looked back at Jessica.

"It sure is," said my sister.

"Oh, wonderful." The alien who had my body seemed relieved. "Please forgive me for barging in like this, but I found his name and address on this card."

The alien who had my body held out one of the phony ID cards my friends and I bought in the city when we were in sixth grade.

"I'm afraid it's gotten dark outside and I'm frightfully cold," the alien who had my body went on. "I don't know anyone, and I have no place to go. If it wouldn't be a horrible imposition, I was wondering if I might be able to take shelter here for the evening?"

Was he serious? I stepped out from behind Josh and Andy. "You'd better believe you can take shelter here, bud," I squeaked.

"My word!" exclaimed the alien who had my body. He spun around as if he was going to run away into the dark. In a flash, I stretched out my alien arms and grabbed his ankles.

Yikes! The next thing I knew, he yanked me right off my stubby alien legs and started to drag me out the door behind him.

"Help!" I shrieked as he dragged me into the dark. I still had a grip on his legs, but I wasn't strong enough to stop him.

"Josh! Andy!" I shouted as he dragged me across the stiff, frozen grass in my front yard. With my alien mitten-hands around his ankles, I was able to slow him down enough for my friends to catch up to us.

"Oooof!" The alien who had my body crashed to the lawn as Josh and Andy tackled him.

"Let me go, I say!" The alien who had my body tried to fight his way out of my friends' grasp. "Let me go, you ruffians!"

He kicked and struggled, but Josh and Andy finally got him to calm down by sitting on him.

"You have no right to do this, you barbarians!"

the alien who had my body shouted. "It's a free country! This is a violation of my civil rights! I'm being illegally detained!"

"How do you know about civil rights?" asked Jessica, who'd come out of the house. "Do they have them on your planet, too?"

The alien who had my body suddenly grew quiet.

I let go of his ankles and got up from the frigid ground. "Let's get him back in the house. It's too cold out here."

Twisting the alien's arm behind his back, Josh got him to stand up and go into the house. Inside, I got some bungee cords from the front closet. Andy used them to tie up the alien's hands and feet.

We sat him down on the living room couch. Josh, Andy, and Jessica kept glancing back and forth between the alien who had my body, and me in his. Meanwhile, the alien gazed around the living room.

It felt really eerie when he leveled his gaze at me. I mean, imagine looking at yourself in a mirror. You blink, but the person in the mirror doesn't blink back.

"You shouldn't have taken my body," I squeaked angrily. "It was a totally low, dirtball thing to do."

I wondered if the alien who had my body would

get angry and start yelling. But he only nodded.

"I can understand that you might be perturbed," he replied. "Please accept my apologies. But you must admit that compared to my body, yours is quite splendid. I simply couldn't help myself."

"Why do you talk that way?" Andy asked him.

The alien who had my body scowled. "What way?"

"Using all those big words and talking so proper," Andy explained.

"That's simply the way I speak," replied the alien who had my body.

"It's not like he's spent a lot of time hanging around with us," Josh observed.

The alien who had my body brightened. "I should really love to do that. I mean, hang around with you fellows. I'm sure we'd all have a delightful time."

"Right," I replied suspiciously. "Next you'll want us to untie the bungee cords."

The alien who had my body nodded at his bound-up hands and feet. "Well, truthfully, this is rather uncomfortable."

I turned to my friends. "Don't you see what he's doing? He's trying to act friendly so that we'll untie him. But the second we do, he'll be out of here."

"Oh, no, I'd never do that," protested the alien who had my body.

"Oh, yeah?" I squeaked. "Then how come you tried to run away just now?"

The alien who had my body winced slightly. "It's difficult to explain. If only you could understand what it's like for me to be here. It's just so marvelous! Just look at this room. So many colors and details. Such diverse textures. It's simply outstanding."

The rest of us glanced around.

"Looks like your basic living room to me," Josh said.

"Don't they have living rooms where you come from?" Jessica asked.

The alien who had my body gazed back at her sadly and shook his head. "There's nothing where I come from. Only drab ugliness in varying shades of gray. Ugly square gray houses with ugly square gray rooms. Ugly grayish-green plants and ugly grayish-pink animals. There's no color, no texture. It's . . . it's absolutely abysmal."

"What a bummer," Andy muttered sympathetically.

"Yes." The alien who had my body nodded woefully. "It is quite a bummer. A bummer of immense proportions." He looked at a small bowl of plastic fruit on the coffee table. "Do you see the color and richness in that bowl of fruit? We have nothing like that. It is the most beautiful thing I've ever seen."

"Plastic fruit?" Jessica looked puzzled. "It's totally tacky."

"You don't understand," sighed the alien in my body. "But then, how could you? How could I expect you to believe that where I come from you would be the most beautiful person anyone had ever encountered?"

Jessica looked startled. "Really?"

"Without question," the alien who had my body went on. "I mean, the softness and rosy hue of your skin. The rich fullness of your hair and the heavenly tint of your eyes. Where I come from, you would be worshipped as a goddess."

Andy leaned over to Josh and me and whispered, "Wow, he really does come from an ugly planet!"

Jessica didn't hear him. She was too busy soaking up the alien's compliments. She had a dreamy look on her face, so it was obvious she believed him. But I didn't. I knew he was just trying to butter her up and get her to untie him. Once she did, I'd probably never see my body again.

"Hey, Mr. Body Thief," I squeaked, trying to think of a way to distract them. "Want to see something *really* beautiful?"

"I'd love to." The alien who had my body nodded eagerly.

I got up and started toward the den. If that alien thought my sister and a dumb bowl of fake fruit were beautiful, just wait until he saw our brand-new giant-screen TV with eighty-six cable channels!

Behind me, Josh and Andy slid their arms through the arms of the alien who had my body and helped him up.

As I went toward the den, I noticed that I could walk a little farther and a little faster on my stubby alien legs. It seemed that each time I used them, they got a bit stronger and less tired.

It reminded me of when I broke my arm and had to have a cast. After the cast came off, my arm felt really weak. But the more I used it, the stronger it got. That made me wonder if the alien came from a planet where people rarely used their legs.

At the entrance to the den, I stretched my alien arm out and reached for the TV remote. It was funny how the remote fit perfectly into my alien mitten-hand. And with the alien's extra-long flexible thumb, I was able to hit every button on the remote perfectly.

The TV screen was just flashing on when Josh and Andy brought in the alien who had my body. I flipped through the channels to an old episode of *Beavis and Butt-Head* on MTV. I turned up the volume.

"How's *this* for something *really* beautiful?" I squeaked proudly.

The alien who had my body froze. His eyes

bulged and his mouth fell open. His skin went pale.

"Yaaahhhhhhhhhhhhhhhhhhhhhh!" He let out a scream so loud I had to cover my floppy alien ears.

20

The next thing I knew, the alien who had my body twisted free of Josh and Andy and fell to the floor. Even though his hands and feet were still bound with bungee cords, he began to inch through the living room on his knees and elbows like a giant caterpillar.

"Get him!" I squeaked.

Josh and Andy had no trouble grabbing him. With his hands and feet tied, he couldn't get far. Once again they sat on him.

"I knew it!" I squeaked at the alien who had my body. "You were just trying to catch us off guard and escape."

"No!" he yelped. Scrunched under the weight of Josh and Andy, he was trembling and pale.

"*Uhhhhhh . . . Uhhhhh . . . Uhhhh . . .*" From the den came the sounds of *Beavis and Butt-Head.*

The alien who had my body twisted and

squirmed. "Turn it off!" he cried. "I beg you. Have mercy! Turn it off!"

Even with the alien's hands and feet tied, Josh and Andy were having trouble holding him down.

"He's really spazzing out!" Andy warned.

"Better turn off the TV, Jake," grunted Josh.

I pushed the power button on the remote and the TV went off. The alien who had my body stopped struggling and collapsed in an exhausted heap. His hair was damp with sweat and he was panting for breath.

Jessica kneeled down on the carpet beside him and straightened his hair. "Everything's going to be okay," she said soothingly. "We won't turn it on again, I promise."

"Thank you," he wheezed. "I'll be forever grateful."

Jessica looked up at me. "I don't think he was trying to escape, Jake. I really think there's something about the TV that freaked him out."

Having reached the same conclusion, I nodded and felt kind of bad. "It's not like I made him watch on purpose."

"I know," Jessica said. "I just don't think it's very nice to constantly accuse him of trying to escape. I believe him, Jake. I think if you came from the kind of ugly place he comes from . . . and had his funny-looking body . . ."

"I *do* have his funny-looking body," I reminded her.

"Well," Jessica continued, "then you wouldn't want to go back there, either."

I knew she was right, but I was nervous. Wherever he came from sounded really bad. I was still worried that if the alien got away again with my body, I'd never get it back.

Meanwhile, the alien who had my body had calmed down.

"I think it's safe to let him go," Jessica told Josh and Andy.

Josh and Andy got off him. The alien who had my body sat up. Andy sat on the floor beside him. "Can I ask you a question?"

The alien who had my body nodded.

"In your travels through space, have you ever come across any giant aliens with really big nostrils?" Andy asked.

The alien who had my body scowled. "Why do you ask?"

"Well, I have this theory that meteorites are actually giant petrified space goobers," Andy explained. "But in order for my theory to work, there have to be giant aliens with really big nostrils."

The alien who had my body stared at Andy as if he'd lost his mind.

"On second thought, maybe this is the wrong time to talk about it," Andy said.

"Especially since we have to get home," added Josh.

Andy got up from the floor. He and Josh headed for the front door. I went with them and waited while they zipped up their jackets.

"Listen, Jake, I really hope you'll think about being goalie tomorrow," Josh said.

"Yeah," Andy agreed. "With those long arms, we'll rule."

"I can't," I squeaked. "Who'll watch the alien and make sure he doesn't run away while I'm playing? Besides, it's a county league. Aliens aren't allowed. I'll be disqualified."

Josh and Andy glanced silently at each other as if they were trying to come up with an answer.

"I know!" Andy said. "You can wear my scarf! People won't see you."

"But I can't wear sunglasses and a hat," I squeaked. "That's not allowed, either."

"I'll bet you could wear a face mask," Josh said.

"Right," agreed Andy. "Like the kind we wear snow-boarding. It'll be so cold they'll have to allow it."

Andy and Josh were really serious about me playing goalie.

"I hate to burst your bubble, guys, but it's not going to happen," I squeaked. "I have to keep an eye on this alien."

Andy's shoulders sagged with disappointment.

Josh looked down at the floor and pursed his lips. "Just think about it, okay?"

"Yeah," said Andy. "This could be the start of a new career, Jake. Maybe you could be a professional soccer goalie and travel with the circus during the off season."

"Drop dead," I grumbled.

21

Josh and Andy left, and I went back to the living room. But Jessica and the alien who had my body weren't there. Then I heard sounds coming from the kitchen.

"For a while I was into this vegetarian thing," my sister was saying. "But I'm over that now. Do they have vegetarians where you come from?"

I stuck my alien head into the kitchen. Jessica was standing at the stove, stirring a steaming pot with a wooden spoon. The alien who had my body was sitting at the kitchen table. I couldn't believe it! My sister had untied his hands and feet!

"Like everything else where I come from, the food is always dull, grayish, and bland," the alien who had my body replied. "It hardly has any taste at all."

"What a drag." Jessica sprinkled some spices into the pot. "I'm doing hot and spicy now. I'm really into flavor in a major way."

"Sounds wonderful," the alien who had my body said with a smile.

"Uh, could I speak to you in private for a second?" I squeaked at my sister.

"I'm in the middle of a risotto," Jessica answered. "Can't it wait, Jake?"

"No, it *can't* wait," I sputtered. "I have to talk to you *now!*"

Jessica frowned. "Why do you always have to be so demanding?"

"Look at me!" I hissed, hoping the alien couldn't hear. "You'd be demanding, too, if you were stuck in this miserable body! All I'm asking is that you step out into the hall for a moment. It's the *least* you could do."

My sister rolled her eyes to let me know I was being a total pain. Then she turned to the alien who had my body. "Would you excuse me for a moment?"

"Of course," he replied.

My sister came out into the hall.

"What are you doing?" I whispered.

"Cooking him dinner," Jessica said.

"Why?" I asked.

"Because he just took a long trip," she answered. "He must be hungry."

"Why in the world did you untie him? Now he can escape."

"And go where?" Jessica asked.

"Anywhere," I squeaked. "Alaska ... China ... even the moon."

Jessica shook her head. "I don't think he'll do that. I think he likes it here."

"How do you know that?" I asked in disbelief. "He's an alien, for Pete's sake."

"It's just a feeling I get," Jessica replied. "Now please don't upset him. He's just been through a very traumatic experience."

"*He's* been through a traumatic experience?" I repeated in disbelief. "What about me? He stole my body."

"No, he didn't," Jessica said. "It was an accident. And I'm sure he'll give it back when the time is right."

"How can you be so sure of that?" I asked.

"I just am," Jessica replied simply. "I feel like I can trust him. Now I really have to get back into the kitchen before my risotto burns."

My sister went back into the kitchen.

I couldn't believe it.

Since when can you trust an alien?

22

Back in the kitchen, the alien who had my body offered to help my sister cook dinner.

"That's very nice of you," Jessica replied. "But it's not necessary. Uh . . . you don't happen to have a name, do you?"

The alien who had my body looked surprised. "Oh, dear, how rude of me. Of course I have a name. It's Howard."

"Howard?" my sister repeated with a frown.

"Why, yes, is there something wrong with that?" asked the alien who had my body.

"Well, no, of course not," Jessica stammered. "It's just that . . ."

"Just what?" asked Howard.

Jessica gave me a sideways glance. I knew what she was thinking.

"What my sister's trying to say," I squeaked, "is that since you don't come from around here, we expected you to have a far-out name. Something like Frimgle, or Neemoid, or Pavement."

"Sorry to disappoint you," Howard the alien said with a wry smile.

"Where did you learn to speak English so well?" Jessica said.

"It's just something I picked up," Howard the alien answered, joining Jessica at the stove. "Please, there must be something I can do to assist."

"You really don't have to," Jessica said. "If I need anything, Jake can do it."

"Gee, thanks," I grumbled.

"But I insist," said Howard the alien. "You're cooking this wonderful meal. Can't I help?"

"Believe me, this is nothing," Jessica replied. "I love to cook. And I'm looking forward to serving someone who actually appreciates fine food."

She turned and gave me a quick sneer, which Howard didn't see.

"Well, at least let me set the table," said Howard the alien.

He moved away from the stove and started looking through the kitchen cabinets.

"The plates and glasses are over there," Jessica said, pointing.

Howard the alien took out some plates and glasses. It seemed a little strange to me that he knew how to speak English and knew that we Earthlings needed plates and glasses to eat. Was it possible that wherever he came from, they ate in exactly the same way we did?

Finally dinner was ready. Jessica placed a bowl

of steaming hot risotto on the table in front of us. It was all mushed together and looked pretty gross to me, but Howard the alien leaned over the bowl and took a long, deep sniff. "That smells fantastic!"

"Just wait until you taste it." Jessica beamed happily. She spooned big globs of the stuff onto our plates.

I stared down at the glob on my plate. It was sort of yellowish and lumpy with specks of red and green in it. Like something the dog had barfed up.

Of course Mr. Wonderful Alien picked up his fork and started to wolf it down as if he hadn't seen food in years.

"Marvelous!" he mumbled as he ate. "Divine! Fabulous!"

Jessica positively glowed. "Finally! Someone around here who appreciates fine food!"

I got up and made myself a peanut butter and jelly sandwich. Meanwhile Howard the alien had seconds . . .

And then thirds!

Finally he was finished. "My compliments to the chef," he said, dabbing his lips with a napkin.

Jessica smiled broadly.

"You know what's really amazing?" I squeaked.

"What?" Jessica shot me a dirty look as if she sensed that I was going to say something upsetting. I also got the feeling she would have been very happy if Howard the alien kept my body forever and I just disappeared.

"That we're sitting here having dinner with someone from another planet," I squeaked, turning to Howard the alien. "I mean, how did you know we needed plates and glasses? Where did you learn how to use a fork? Is it the same on your planet?"

Howard the alien looked a little startled. Then he smiled. "It's all very logical, really."

"What happened before with the TV?" I squeaked. "I mean, you really freaked out."

Howard stopped smiling. He slouched a little in his chair and began to look glum.

"Oh, you don't have to answer if you don't want to," Jessica quickly said. "It's really none of our business."

"I suppose I do owe you an explanation," Howard the alien replied wistfully. "You see, where I come from we also have television. In fact, it's just about all we have anymore. Watching TV is all people do."

Jessica gave me a knowing look.

"What's interesting is that I've seen old pictures of our ancestors and they look remarkably like you," Howard the alien went on. "But look at me now."

Both he and Jessica looked at *me* since I was occupying his body.

"Do you know why my legs are so short and

weak?" Howard asked. "It's because we hardly ever go anywhere. All we do is sit and watch TV."

"Is that why your arms can stretch so far?" Jessica asked.

Howard the alien nodded my head. "Exactly. Our arms let us reach for everything we need without getting up."

"What about your voice?" I squeaked.

"It's in the process of fading away," Howard the alien explained. "No one talks to anyone anymore. We all just sit and stare."

Jessica turned to me. "I'm sure you can relate to that, right, Jake?"

"Precisely," Howard the alien replied sadly.

"Is your skin so pale because you never go outside?" Jessica guessed.

"And are these big eyes for seeing the TV screen better?" I added.

Howard the alien nodded.

"But what about this beak mouth?" I squeaked. "How does that fit into watching TV all the time?"

"It's perfect for tearing open plastic bags of junk food," Howard the alien replied. "I know my body looks terrible, but it's quite well suited for the environment I live in."

I blinked in astonishment. "That's exactly what Mr. Dirksen always says!"

"Let it be a warning," Jessica said to me.

"Forget it," I squeaked. "I know we watch a lot of TV and eat a lot of junk food, but I can't believe we'll ever look as bad as Howard. No offense or anything."

Howard smiled back sadly. "Maybe now you can understand why I tried to escape when I found myself occupying your body. You can't imagine how exhilarating it felt to go outside. To be able to move about freely. To experience all the color this world offers, and to smell the fresh air. I mean, just to see the beauty in a single blade of grass was extraordinary."

Without warning my sister burst into tears. "Please stop!" she begged. "You're making me feel so bad."

Howard the alien apologized over and over again until Jessica stopped crying and dabbed her tears away with a napkin.

"I'm terribly sorry," Howard the alien said. "I never meant to make you feel bad. I just hope you truly appreciate what you have."

"You're right." Jessica nodded. "You're really right. I feel like taking that new giant-screen TV of ours and throwing it out."

The next thing I knew, Jessica jumped up and headed for the den.

"Wait!" I squeaked.

23

I raced into the den as fast as those stubby alien legs would carry me and managed to get between my sister and the TV. I stretched my alien arms protectively across the TV screen.

"Don't do anything you'll regret," I warned her. "Dad'll have a fit if you hurt this thing."

"I'm not so sure," Jessica replied.

"Look, I'm not saying I totally disagree with Howard," I squeaked. "I just don't think things will ever go *that* far here. I mean, even you like to watch a TV show once in a while."

Jessica let out a big sigh. Then she nodded and went back to the kitchen. I breathed a little easier. *Phew!* That was close! I lovingly wiped my alien mitten marks off the screen, then followed.

Back in the kitchen, Howard the alien picked up his plate and started toward the sink. "To show you how much I appreciate your cooking, Jessica, I shall do the dishes."

"No way," Jessica replied. "You're our guest. You should relax. Jake will do the dishes."

"Gee, thanks," I muttered.

"But I insist," Howard the alien protested. "I haven't done anything to help."

"It doesn't matter," Jessica said. "You know what? I want you to come with me. There's something I want to show you."

Jessica led Howard the alien out of the kitchen. Being curious about where they were going, I started to follow. But my sister shook her head. "You're doing the dishes, remember?"

Normally I would have told her to get stuffed, but this time I didn't. Maybe because I knew I would also be doing the dishes for Howard the alien. And the truth was, I did feel kind of bad for him. Besides, doing the dishes in Howard's body was easy. With his long arms I could clear them off the table without even leaving the kitchen sink.

A few moments later, Jessica came back into the kitchen.

"Where'd you take him?" I asked as I started rinsing the dishes and putting them in the dishwasher.

"Into the den," she said. "I wanted him to see Mom's collection of art books."

"You mean those big boring books filled with paintings?" I asked.

Jessica nodded. "He thinks they're the most beautiful things he's ever seen."

"He thinks *everything* is the most beautiful thing he's ever seen," I reminded her. I held up a dirty plate. "Behold, the beauty of a crusty plate. Consider the magnificent crud stuck to it."

"You're being totally mean," my sister said.

"I know," I admitted. "I probably wouldn't feel this way if I had my own body back. You didn't happen to talk to him about giving it back, did you?"

"No, but I do want to talk to you about it," Jessica said.

There was something about the tone of her voice that made me nervous. "Don't tell me you want me to stay in this yucky body!"

"Well, it did cross my mind," my sister admitted.

"Get real!" I growled.

"He is awfully nice," Jessica said.

"Oh, yeah? What do you think Mom and Dad would do if they came home and found out that you let an alien have my body?" I asked.

"Well . . ." Jessica gave me a sly smile. "They'd probably raise my allowance."

"Very funny," I muttered. "I wonder how you'd like it if some disgusting-looking alien stole *your* body."

"I wouldn't like it, silly," Jessica said, getting serious. "I know it's not fair. But here's what I'm thinking. Mr. Dirksen won't be back until tomorrow night, so the earliest you can go back into school and switch is Monday morning, right?"

"Right," I squeaked.

"And you've seen how much Howard appreciates being in your body, haven't you?"

I eyed her suspiciously. "If you're trying to talk me into letting Howard stay in my body *one second* longer than he has to, you can forget it."

"No, I'm not saying that," Jessica said. "But here's what I'm thinking. We both know how incredibly thrilling it is for him to be here. So instead of keeping him locked up in the house tomorrow, why not let him enjoy our world for one more day?"

"What if he tries to escape?" I asked.

"I really don't think he will," Jessica said. "I promise I'll spend the whole day with him just to make sure."

"Why?" I asked.

"Because I feel terrible for him, Jake," my sister said. "His life sounds so awful. Don't you feel bad for him?"

"Well, sort of," I had to admit. "But I'd feel a lot more sympathy if he was in someone else's body."

"I swear I'll stay with him all day," Jessica promised. "I'll take him places he'll enjoy. In the meantime, you can play goalie for the soccer team. You'll be the hero who saves the day while

Alex Silver sits on the sidelines with his twisted ankle."

The hero . . . I hadn't thought of that. Jessica was right. It did sound pretty good.

"You swear you'll both be here on Monday morning so we can make the switch?" I asked.

"Absolutely," Jessica said.

"Even though you like him in my body more than you like me?"

Jessica nodded. "He's nice, Jake. But I'd never be able to live with myself if I didn't help you get back into your own body."

24

Jessica and I went to break the news to Howard. In the den, our new friend was no longer looking at my mom's art books. Instead, he was sitting at the desk, typing on my dad's electric typewriter.

"What are you doing?" Jessica asked.

"Assisting your brother with his report," Howard the alien replied, and gestured at the report in my open notebook. "You see, Jake, there's substantial evidence supporting the possibility of life on other planets. I don't want to see you get a bad grade."

He was doing my report! I couldn't believe it. "Hey, way to go, dude."

"Howard, really, you *don't* have to do my brother's homework." Jessica had to butt in.

"Why not?" I asked. "I mean, it's not like I asked him. If this is what he feels like doing, I say, go with the flow."

"I'll only be a moment more," Howard the alien

said, and started typing again. My sister and I watched in amazement as he made my fingers fly over the typewriter keys.

"How in the world did you learn to type like that?" Jessica asked.

"Oh, uh, I don't know. It just comes naturally, I guess." Howard stopped typing and seemed a little flustered.

"Hey, it's cool," I squeaked. "You're obviously an alien of many talents. Don't stop typing."

We watched as Howard the alien finished my report. He pulled the sheet of paper out of the typewriter and handed it to me. "I think your teacher will be much happier with this."

"Wow, thanks, dude," I squeaked.

"And now we have good news for *you*," said Jessica. "Instead of making you stay in the house all day tomorrow, I'm going to take you anywhere you want. Anywhere around here, that is."

Howard blinked in astonishment. "You mean, we could go to a bookstore or a museum?"

"Whatever you want," Jessica said.

"There's a cool video arcade at the mall," I suggested. "And you have to check out the skateboards at Maximum Pro-Fit Sports."

Tears began to fall out of Howard's eyes and run down his cheeks. It was kind of weird because I'd never seen myself cry before.

"I don't know what to say," Howard blubbered.

"I'm speechless. Oh, thank you so very, very much!"

He jumped up, hugged my sister, and gave her a big kiss on the cheek. Then he turned to me.

"Whoa!" I held up my alien mitten-hands to stop him. "Let's not go overboard. On this planet, most guys don't kiss each other."

Howard the alien smiled and wiped the tears off his cheeks. Then he turned to Jessica. "What about the Jeffersonville Art Museum? Could we go there?"

"Sure thing," my sister answered.

While my sister made plans with Howard the alien, I called Josh and told him I'd play goalie the next day.

"Great," Josh said over the phone. "What made you change your mind?"

"If you can't use the body you like, you might as well like the body you use," I replied.

There was a moment of silence over the phone. Then Josh cleared his throat. "Whatever you say, Jake."

25

At breakfast the next morning, the radio reported that it was the coldest November day in thirty years. And even windier than the day before. Through the kitchen window, I saw people bundled up and holding on to their hats to keep them from flying off. Their scarves flapped behind them in the breeze.

"Fabulous! Simply fabulous!" Howard the alien gushed as he started on his second helping of blueberry pancakes with strawberry syrup.

Meanwhile, I was filling my alien stomach with plain pancakes. Jessica was in such a good mood that she'd made both kinds that morning.

"These are pretty good, too," I complimented my sister, then drenched my pancakes with regular syrup.

Jessica beamed. "If you really want to try something good, Jake, you should try *real* maple syrup instead of that fake concoction of sugar syrup and food coloring."

"You mean, the stuff they make from *tree sap*?" I shook my head. "Forget it."

Jessica smirked. "You will always be hopeless, no matter *whose* body you're in."

Suddenly I saw something strange on the sidewalk outside. Two people passed our house on those motorized three-wheeled scooter chairs you sometimes see old people using. They were completely bundled up, but I still couldn't help wondering why such frail-looking people would go out on such a cold day.

"Have you ever seen those two before?" I asked Jessica.

She looked out the window and shook her head. "Never. I wonder where they're going."

Howard the alien leaned over and looked out the window. Suddenly the blood drained from his face. "Oh, my word!" He jumped up and pulled the curtains shut.

"What's wrong?" Jessica asked, alarmed.

"It's them!" Howard the alien gasped. "They've come to get me!"

"Who?" I asked.

"They're from my planet," Howard the alien said.

"They want to take you back?" Jessica guessed.

"Yes," said Howard the alien.

"Did they see you?" I asked.

"Not yet." Howard's lower lip trembled. "But they'll be back. Now that they know I'm around here, they won't stop looking until they find me."

Then it hit me. Howard the alien had my body! If they took him back, they'd have to take my body, too. That meant I'd *never* get my body back!

"We have to hide you," I squeaked in a panic.

"No." Howard the alien shook his head. "We have to hide *you*. Because if they see you in my body, they'll assume you're me."

I felt my alien jaw drop.

He was right. "And then they'll take me back to that horrible place!" I realized.

"Don't panic," Howard the alien said.

"That's easy for you to say!" I shrieked. "If they find us, you're not going anywhere. I'm the one who'll go."

"No." Howard the alien shook his head. "I'd never let that happen. I'd tell them that we exchanged bodies."

"Why should they believe you?" I asked nervously.

"Because they will," Howard the alien said. "You'll just have to trust me."

He parted the curtains slightly and peeked out. "You see that box the one on the right is carrying?"

Jessica and I peeked out. I could see a small gray plastic thing in the alien's lap. It looked like an old Game Boy.

"It's a super-nimble integrated fragrance-finding electronic resonator," Howard the alien said. "Otherwise known as a SNIFFER. It can follow virtually undetectable scents."

"Including the scent of an alien?" I guessed.

"Precisely," Howard the alien replied.

"Then what do we do?" I asked.

"We must mask your scent."

26

Jessica was all too happy to provide the perfume. It smelled totally yucky, flowery-sweet, but at least it wasn't that gross patchouli oil she used to wear.

After I put it on, Howard the alien took a deep sniff. "Excellent," he said. "Now it will be impossible for the SNIFFER to locate you."

"But they'll still be able to see me," I squeaked.

"No," said Howard the alien. "You'll be dressed in heavy clothing. You'll resemble every other person out there today."

"Only shorter," added Jessica.

"And they certainly won't expect you to be walking around on your own legs, much less playing soccer," Howard the alien said.

Jessica checked her watch. "It's time to go to the museum."

"Wait!" I blurted nervously. "You're not just going to leave me here alone, are you?"

Howard the alien and my sister exchanged a look.

"I assure you that you'll be safe," Howard said. "But just to be certain, I suggest you stay inside until your game begins. Jessica and I will visit the museum this morning and then join you at the game. We'll be there to keep an eye on things."

I had an intense desire to bite my lip nervously, but when you've got a beak, you can't really do it. "You're absolutely, totally, completely, cross-your-heart-and-hope-to-die *sure* this will work?"

"Yes," said Howard the alien. "I'm positive we can get away with it for at least one day."

27

Howard the alien and Jessica went to the museum, and I watched TV all morning. I really didn't see what was so bad about TV. Sure I watched a lot, but I did other stuff, too. I played basketball and football and soccer with my friends. I played CD games on my computer. And at least once a year I read a book for school.

Around noon the doorbell rang. I went to answer it dressed in my soccer uniform. In the attic I'd found a pair of old cleats for my little alien feet, and small shin guards for my stubby alien legs. But the only jersey and shorts I had were the ones for the human body Howard was now in.

I pulled open the front door. Josh and Andy came in, bundled in sweats, coats, hats, and scarves.

When they saw me, they started to grin.

"What's so funny?" I asked.

"Oh, I don't know," Andy mumbled. He was

pressing his lips tightly together in an effort not to laugh.

I gave Josh a questioning look. He had clamped his hands over his mouth, but his face was turning red.

"Look, if this is the way you guys are going to be, maybe I won't play after all," I squeaked angrily.

"No, please!" Josh fell to his knees and clasped his hands together. "We're trying not to laugh. *Really!*"

"It's just that —" Andy blurted, then stopped himself.

"It's just what?" I demanded.

Andy pointed at my feet. "Your shorts are almost touching the ground!"

I looked down. On my dumb alien body my shorts looked like baggy nylon pants hanging down to the tops of my cleats.

By rolling them up at the waist, I was able to make them shorter. "Is that better?" I asked.

Josh and Andy shared a doubtful look.

"You'd better wear a lot of clothes so no one gets a good look at you," Josh said.

Meanwhile, Andy sniffed the air and wrinkled his nose. "Jessica sure put on a lot of perfume this morning."

"It's not Jessica," I squeaked. "It's me."

"You?" Josh frowned. "Why are you wearing perfume?"

"Because Howard said I should."

Andy made a face. "Howard who?"

"The alien dude who has my body," I explained.

"His name is *Howard*!?" Josh asked in disbelief.

"Yeah," I squeaked. "It was a real disappointment. I was expecting something like Poopah the Quonset Hut."

"So what's with the perfume?" Andy asked.

"It's the only way to keep the other aliens from finding me," I explained.

"What other aliens?" Josh asked.

"The ones on the three-wheeled scooter chairs. They've got a super-nimble integrated fragrance-finding electronic resonator, otherwise known as a SNIFFER. If I don't wear perfume, they'll find me."

Josh and Andy looked at each other.

"Sounds like it's straitjacket time," Josh said.

"I'm not sure they make one small enough to fit him," Andy replied.

"You just want to call the nuthouse and have them come and get him?" Josh asked.

"Can't we wait until *after* the game?" asked Andy.

"You really think he's mentally capable of playing soccer?" Josh asked.

"Worse comes to worst, we take off his face mask and let the other team see what he really looks like," Andy said. "Maybe they'll start laughing so hard they won't be able to kick straight."

"I'm not crazy, guys," I squeaked.

"Oh, I definitely agree," Andy said. "You're not crazy, Jake. You're just totally, one-hundred-and-twenty-percent psycho."

I shook my alien head. "Everything I told you is true."

Josh and Andy both gave me doubtful looks.

"I'm serious," I insisted.

"Okay, I'm going to give you a test to see if you're sane," Josh said. "Pretend you're going to spend the next twenty years alone on a tropical island. Which of the following would you take with you? A) All the great books. B) The five most beautiful babes in the world. C) A twenty-year supply of Pop-Tarts variety packs."

I thought about it.

At first the answer seemed too obvious.

Then I realized why.

"It's a trick question," I squeaked. "Because after a while the Pop Tarts would get stale, or bugs would get into them."

Josh turned to Andy and shrugged. "I guess he's sane."

"So why'd you have to use perfume?" Andy asked me.

"What else was I supposed to use?" I asked.

"Something *manly*," Andy said. "Like B.O. in a bottle."

"Look, it doesn't matter now," Josh said. "Let's just get to the game."

"Let me get my parka," I said, heading for the closet.

Andy reached into his pocket and took out a black face mask. "And wear this."

I pulled on my sweats, parka, hat, scarf, mittens, and Andy's ski mask. By the time I was finished, I felt like a little kid bundled in a snowsuit.

Josh, Andy, and I left my house. Outside the air was as cold as ice, but I was warm with all those layers on. Gusts of wind made the leaves swirl around in the street and caused the bare tree branches to sway and creak.

"Want to know who's going to win the soccer game today?" Josh asked through chattering teeth as we struggled to walk against the wind. "The team that doesn't freeze to death."

I was about to add that the wind would probably blow us off the field first. But just then two figures came around the corner and started down the sidewalk toward us.

They were both bundled in black and riding those three-wheeled scooters.

Aliens!

28

"It's *them*!" I whispered.

Andy stopped. "Who?"

"The aliens!"

My friends stared down the sidewalk at the approaching scooters.

"See that small gray thing that looks like a Game Boy?" I whispered. "That's the SNIFFER."

"Maybe we'd better run." Andy started to turn.

"No." Josh grabbed his arm. "If we do they'll know something's wrong."

"But what about the SNIFFER?" Andy reminded him.

"Just stay cool," Josh whispered.

The two aliens on the three-wheeled scooter chairs came closer. What if the SNIFFER detected my alien scent under Jessica's perfume? What if they captured me and took me back to the ugly gray planet where all the people did all day was watch TV?

Well, *that* wasn't so bad. . . .

But I'd miss my friends.

The scooters were only a dozen feet away now. I could feel alien goose bumps rise on my alien arms and my alien chest grew tight with fear.

Beep! Beep! Beep! The SNIFFER's alarm went off!

29

My friends and I froze. The aliens stopped their scooter chairs.

We were face-to-face.

Beep! Beep! Beep! The SNIFFER was going crazy.

The aliens looked at one another, then back at us. They reached up and pulled down their scarves just enough to let their nose stubs poke out. Both took a deep sniff.

"Smells bogus," one of them squeaked.

The other held up the SNIFFER and shook it. "Demento machine must be whacked."

"Want to lose it?" asked the first.

"Naw, let's get back on the case," said the other.

They covered up their nose stubs, then drove their scooter chairs around us and continued down the sidewalk.

My friends and I watched them go.

"Did you hear the way they talked?" Andy asked. "They sounded just like us."

"Maybe that's the way they talk on that planet," Josh said.

"It's not the way the alien who has my body speaks," I squeaked.

"Look, who cares?" Josh asked. "The only thing that matters is that we got away with it. Let's get out of here before they change their minds."

We started down the sidewalk again. Andy and Josh walked faster than before. I huffed and puffed as I followed on my stubby alien legs. But I kept thinking about those two aliens and the way they spoke. I had the strangest feeling that something even weirder than aliens was going on.

30

When we got to the field, our team was crowded around Coach Roberts. Not only were our teammates all bundled up, but some had even brought blankets to wrap around themselves when they weren't playing. Coach Roberts was wearing a long, heavy coat with a fur-lined hood. He looked more like an Arctic explorer than a soccer coach.

"Where's Jake?" he asked when he saw us coming. "Alex is still hurt. We need our backup goalie."

"Uh, Jake couldn't make it," Josh said. "So we brought . . . er . . . Brice instead."

Coach Roberts looked down at me and frowned.

"He's new in town," Andy said.

"Have you ever played goalie before?" Coach Roberts asked me.

Hidden under that face mask and all those

clothes, I nodded. I didn't want to speak in front of the team because I was afraid they'd laugh at my squeaky voice.

"He comes from a country where soccer is the national sport," Josh said. "They're small but very quick."

Coach Roberts turned to Andy and Josh. "Can't he speak for himself?"

"Uh, in his country they don't say much," Josh answered.

"They believe in action, not words," Andy chirped in.

"Well, I guess action is what's going to count today," Coach Roberts said, and turned to the rest of the team. "Okay, everyone, time for a warm-up lap. Once around the field and then we'll do some ball-handling drills."

I felt my alien heart drop into my alien stomach. Once around the field on my stubby, weak alien legs?

Andy and Josh gave me helpless looks, then took off to run with the rest of the team around the field.

I lagged way behind and had to stop frequently to catch my breath. By the time I made it all the way around, the team had finished the drills and the game was about to begin.

Coach Roberts gave me a disapproving look. "I thought the people from your country were very quick."

"They are," Andy said, coming to my rescue. "But only over very short distances."

I went out to the goal. It was still freezing cold. Even with all my extra layers of clothes, the wind felt like it was blowing right through me.

Then I saw something that made me feel better. Just as he'd promised, Howard the alien showed up on the sideline with Jessica, to root for us. Howard was so bundled up that Coach Roberts didn't notice that he was in my human body.

The game started. I stood in the goal, hugging myself and shivering, while the midfielders battled for possession of the soccer ball. Every time the other team tried to score, I managed to stop the shot.

By halftime the score was 0–0. Neither team had been able to score. Andy, Josh, and I huddled together with Jessica and Howard the alien.

"Good playing, guys," Jessica said.

"We really lucked out with Jake playing goalie," Josh said in a low voice. "So far he's been able to block every shot."

"I rather agree," said Howard the alien. "I thought you made some first-class stops, Jake. Excellent ball-handling."

That was weird. Howard sounded as if he knew soccer pretty well. I was just about to ask if they played a game like it on his planet when Josh suddenly nudged me.

"Uh-oh," he hissed. "Looks like we've got company."

I spun around. Coming across the field toward us were the two aliens on their scooter chairs!

31

We all stared in shocked silence as the two aliens bumped across the grass toward us on their scooter chairs.

"What are they doing here?" Jessica hissed.

I gave Howard the alien a worried look. "You told me if I wore perfume they wouldn't be able to smell me!"

Andy leaned toward me and sniffed. "I hate to say this, Jake, but you don't smell like perfume anymore."

"Why not?" I squeaked.

"It must be the wind," Jessica guessed. "Perfume wears off anyway, but this wind made it happen faster."

"Then they're going to get me!" I squealed in horror. "They're gonna take me back to the ugly planet!"

Howard the alien bit his lip. And since he had my body, it was my lip he was biting. I was jealous because that was just what I felt like doing.

"This is bad." Josh sounded grim.

"Believe it," I agreed. "You're going to lose your best friend."

"Forget that," said Andy. "If they take you away now we won't have a goalie. We'll lose the game."

"Is that all you care about?" I asked.

"Well, it *is* the championship," Andy said.

Tweeeeeet! Tweeeeeet! The ref blew his whistle, signaling the start of the second half.

"Come on, we have to go back out on the field," Josh said.

"No way," I squeaked. "I'm getting out of here."

"Where're you going to go?" Jessica asked.

I looked at Howard the alien for the answer. But he just shrugged. "I don't know what to tell you," he said. "Without the perfume to mask your scent, the SNIFFER can follow you anywhere."

Meanwhile, the aliens on the scooter chairs were getting closer! Those scooter chairs were going pretty fast, too. I doubted that I could outrun them with my stubby alien legs.

"You mean, no matter where I go, they're gonna catch me?" I squeaked in terror.

"It would be a distinct possibility," Howard the alien replied.

Tweeeeeet! The ref blew his whistle again.

"Come on, boys! Get out on the field!" Coach Roberts shouted.

"That's it!" Josh cried. "I know one place where they won't be able to get you. On the field!"

"He's right," Andy agreed. "There's no way the ref will let them drive those things into the middle of the game."

The aliens were getting closer and I couldn't think of an alternative plan. Being on the field would buy me some time while I figured out what to do next.

I went out to the goal and got ready.

Tweeeeeet! Tweeeeeet! The ref blew his whistle and the second half began.

Tweeeeeet! Almost immediately the ref had to blow his whistle to stop the game. The aliens on the scooter chairs had followed me onto the field!

The ref and the coaches ran toward the aliens, waving their arms and shouting, "Get off the field! We're in the middle of a game!"

The aliens stopped, then turned off the field.

The ref started the game again.

I tried to concentrate on playing, but I couldn't stop watching the aliens out of the corner of my eye. They had parked their scooters on the sideline. Every time I looked in their direction, they'd wave.

It was weird. They didn't seem angry or anything.

Of course, I couldn't see the expressions on their faces because they were covered up. Maybe on their planet waving meant *"We're gonna kill you!"*

The game got really intense during the second half. At first, every time I looked at the aliens, they were looking back at me.

But after a while they stopped looking at me and started watching the game.

Then Andy scored!

A cheer went up from our side of the field. I looked over at the aliens. They were clapping!

Now we were ahead 1–0. The other team knew they had to score or they'd lose the championship. A goal would force the game into a sudden-death overtime where either team could win.

With seconds left in the game, a player from the other team broke free and started dribbling the ball toward me. A second later he kicked.

The ball sailed high in the air.

It was heading for the far corner of the goal.

There was no way any human could reach it.

I dove, and stretched my alien arms out.

They stretched . . .

And stretched . . .

And stretched!

I got just enough of my mitten-hands on the ball to knock it down and stop it from rolling into the goal!

32

A shocked silence fell over the field, as if no one could believe what they'd just seen.

Then came the sound of clapping . . . from the aliens!

As if they were the only ones who could believe it.

And now they knew for certain that I was the one they were looking for!

Tweeeeeet! Tweeeeeet! Tweeeeeet! The ref blew his whistle three times.

It was the end of the game!

We'd won the county championship!

The next thing I knew, Josh and Andy were running toward me.

"You did it!" Josh shouted gleefully. "You saved the game!"

He and Andy lifted me onto their shoulders and carried me back to the sideline.

Everyone crowded around me, congratulating me on the great save.

"That was fantastic, Brice!" Coach Roberts patted me on the shoulder. "You won the championship for us!"

"You're the hero," Andy said.

I should have been happy, but instead I was watching fearfully as the aliens circled the crowd on their scooter chairs, trying to get closer to me.

Jessica and Howard the alien squeezed through the noisy crowd toward me.

"Congratulations," Howard said. "That was a spectacular save."

"Maybe, but who's going to save me?" I asked, nodding at the circling aliens.

"I won't let them take you, Jake," Howard said. "I've enjoyed every second of being in your body, but I know you deserve to get it back. They'll have to wait until tomorrow morning before they take me home."

"But what if they think it's a trick?" I asked.

Howard the alien shook his head. "Believe me, Jake, they won't think that."

The crowd started to thin out as players and their parents hurried to their cars to get out of the cold. Howard turned toward one of the aliens, who was now rolling straight toward us.

Suddenly I felt really bad for Howard. He was a truly nice guy, and anyone could see how much he hated going back.

"Wait!" I called after him. "Maybe we can still get away!"

Just then I felt two long arms go around me from behind.

The other alien had snuck up on me!

I was caught!

33

I thought of crying out for help, but I realized it wouldn't do any good.

Everyone would hear my squeaky voice.

They'd look at me more closely.

They'd see my alien body and think I was an alien.

Then I'd be carted off to a laboratory somewhere and sliced up into little slivers in the name of science.

So I stayed quiet even though those creepy alien arms were wrapped tightly around me. They pulled me close to the alien on the scooter behind me.

"Oh, Howard," the alien squeaked. "When did you learn to play soccer? That was so awesome cool!"

Huh?

The real Howard stepped in front of the alien who was holding me. "Mother," he said, "please let go of him. You've got the wrong person."

34

*M*other?

"What's he talking about?" Josh asked.

"I get the feeling they're Howard's parents," said Jessica, pointing at the aliens.

Jessica, Josh, Andy, and I stared at Howard the alien in disbelief.

So did the two aliens in the scooter chairs.

"What's with you?" the mother alien asked him.

"I'm your son," Howard answered.

"Way bogus," squeaked the father alien. "Howard never had an ugly body like that."

They were talking about my body!

"Who are you calling ugly?" I squeaked at the father alien. "I mean, talk about the pot calling the kettle black!"

"Take a chill pill, Howard," the mother alien squeaked at me. "Your father is simply bugging out on this Earthling dweeb."

"He's not Howard," said Howard the alien. "I am."

"Oh, yeah, right," smirked the father alien. "And I'm Homer Simpson."

"How do you know about Homer Simpson?" Josh asked.

But the alien father ignored him. "Come on, Doris," he squeaked to the alien mother who had her arms around me. "Let's skate before these dork brains blow the whistle on us."

They started to turn their scooter chairs around. They were taking me away!

"Help!" I squeaked.

My friends quickly blocked the scooter chairs.

"Back off, scuzzballs!" The father alien waved the SNIFFER at us as if it were a ray gun. "Or I'll zap all of you into potato salad."

Everyone except Howard started to back away.

"Wait a minute," said Andy. "How do you know about potato salad?"

"Don't be fooled," Howard said to Jessica and my friends. "That's not a weapon. It's a super-nimble integrated fragrance-finding electronic resonator, and it can't hurt you."

The father alien lowered the SNIFFER. "How could you know that? You're an Earthling."

"I already explained it to you, Father," Howard the alien said, "I'm your son, Howard. I came here to interact with Earthling teenagers. By a stroke of fantastic luck I was able to switch bodies with that Earthling." Howard pointed at me in his body. "And I've had an absolutely marvelous time."

I felt the mother alien's arms slide away from me as she turned to Howard in my body. "You're really my son, Howard?" she asked.

"Yes, Mother," Howard the alien who had my body replied. "I'm your son. The one who ran away from home because I was disgusted with our slothful, passive way of life."

"And you really like it here?" the mother alien asked.

"I love it, Mother," Howard the alien replied. "It's so much better in real life than it is when viewed on television."

"Will someone *please* tell me what's going on?" Jessica begged.

35

Howard the alien suggested we all go back to my house and get out of the cold. A little while later, we were sitting around my kitchen table, drinking hot chocolate.

Can you picture it? Me in an alien body. Two aliens in alien bodies. Howard the alien in *my* Earthling body. And Jessica, Josh, and Andy in their regular bodies.

Weird did not *begin* to describe the way I felt.

"I suppose I owe you all an explanation," Howard the alien began. He nodded at the two aliens who were his parents. They looked sort of like older versions of him. Except that one of them had long dark hairs growing out of his nose stubs and fan ears. And the other one was wearing bright red lipstick on her beak.

"This is my mother, Doris, and my father, Melvin," Howard the alien said.

Jessica, Josh, and Andy shared a puzzled look. I knew exactly what they were thinking: *What kind of aliens are named Doris and Melvin?*

"As you've probably gathered," Howard the alien went on, "they've come to Earth to take me home."

"You really had us freaked, Howard," squeaked Doris.

"Yeah, dude," Melvin chimed in. "Just ditching us like that was, like, totally impaired."

Jessica, Josh, Andy, and I exchanged uncomfortable glances.

"Pardon me for asking this, but why do you talk like that?" Josh asked Howard the alien's parents.

"Like what, dude?" replied Melvin.

"Like you're teenagers," Andy said.

"That is so totally not true," squeaked Melvin. "This is how all adults speak on our planet." Then he pointed at Howard. "He's the one who's got, like, the bogus teenage way of talking."

"Didn't it seem bizarre to you that we all sound like your parents?" Jessica asked Howard.

Howard the alien simply shook his head. "Not at all, actually."

"So, like, maybe you'd care to fill us in on why you bailed in the first place," Doris said to Howard.

"You're already familiar with the reason, Mother," Howard answered. "It's because I hate our life."

Melvin the alien father shook his head wearily.

117

"That's such a totally rude thing to say. We happen to have a way cool life."

"It's the most boring life imaginable," Howard grumbled. "All we do is watch TV."

"I really don't get you, Howard," Melvin the alien father sputtered. "Why do you have to be so totally rebellious? Why can't you be like your brothers and sisters? They love vegging out in front of the tube."

Howard suddenly banged his fist on the kitchen table. "Because I want to go outside! I want to run around and play games and breathe fresh air!"

"Back off!" Melvin covered his fan ears with his mitten-hands. "I can't deal with this! It's totally lame!"

"Cool down, dudes!" Doris reached out and placed one mitten-hand on her son's shoulder and the other on her husband's. "Both of you, take a chill pill."

Howard and his father calmed down.

"Get with the program, Melvin," Doris squeaked at her alien husband. "Weren't you, like, completely wowed when we thought it was our son playing in that soccer game?"

"I guess," Melvin the alien father admitted.

"I know I was," Doris the alien mother squeaked.

"And that is precisely what I insist on doing if I come home," Howard the alien stated.

118

"Try to get a grip, hon," Doris the alien said to her son. "We're totally amped about you coming back. And if you're really psyched about going outside, I'm sure we can find a way to cope with it, right, dear?"

Melvin nodded reluctantly. "Sounds totally lame, but I guess we'll try."

36

It was getting late, and Josh and Andy had to go home. Melvin and Doris agreed to stay until the next morning so that I could switch bodies with Howard. They said they were tired from the long trip and wanted to sleep. But Jessica and I stayed up late talking with Howard the alien.

"I just want to thank you both for being so kind to me," Howard said.

"Listen," I squeaked, "if you really don't want to go back, you don't have to. I mean, I do want my body back, but after we switch you're welcome to stay here as long as you want."

"That's very kind of you," Howard replied. "But I think I've made my point with my parents. As much as I love it here, I don't belong. I have an obligation to go back. I feel that I now have a mission in life."

"Are you sure?" I asked, even though I wasn't certain what he was talking about.

"Yes, I'm quite sure," Howard said. "I can see it

very clearly now. There's a great deal of work to be done."

Jessica and I shared a puzzled look.

Briiiiinnnnggg! The phone rang.

"I bet that's Mr. Dirksen," I squeaked, stretching my alien arm across the kitchen to answer it. "Hello?"

"Did you find him?" Mr. Dirksen asked over the phone.

"Yes, he's right here," I squeaked.

"How are you going to get him to school in the morning?" my teacher asked.

"We'll just walk," I squeaked.

"But what if he tries to run away?"

"He won't," I answered.

"Well, okay, if you say so," Mr. Dirksen said. "I'll see you in the morning."

"Definitely," I squeaked and hung up.

Howard yawned. "Oh, dear. I must admit that I'm rather tired after all this excitement."

"And the excitement's not over yet," Jessica said. "We have to get up really early. So maybe we all better bag it for the night."

"Good idea," Howard agreed.

We started to get up, but there was still one thing I wanted to know.

"You never explained why your parents sound like teenagers and you sound like a grown-up," I squeaked.

"Well, it's quite simple, really," said Howard

the alien. "You see, on our planet, we've been watching television for so long that we've grown bored with our own shows. In fact, we've grown so lazy that we don't even produce our own shows anymore. Instead, our equipment is so highly developed that we are able to watch shows from other worlds. And no world in this universe has better shows than Earth."

"You mean, you watch Earth TV on your planet?" Jessica asked.

"Oh, yes," replied Howard. "My parents are particularly fond of *The Simpsons* and *Beavis and Butt-Head.*"

"So that explains why they talk that way!" Jessica realized.

Suddenly it all started to make sense.

"And that's how you knew about soccer and typing and what the plates and glasses were for!" I screeched.

"And what civil rights were!" added Jessica.

"Isn't there *any* show you like to watch?" I asked him.

Howard the alien smiled. "There's one. *Masterpiece Theater.*"

37

The next morning Howard and his parents, and Jessica and I got up at dawn and headed for school. Mr. Dirksen was waiting in his lab for us. My science teacher had a funny look on his face when he saw Howard's mom and dad.

"What's wrong, Mr. Dirksen?" Jessica asked.

Mr. Dirksen blinked as if he were snapping out of a fog. "It's just incredible that we've had extraterrestrial visitors. I wish they didn't have to leave so quickly. There's so much we could learn from each other."

"You already have," said Howard the alien.

Mr. Dirksen scowled. "I have?"

Howard the alien pointed at me in his body. "Jake has," he said.

"I have?" I squeaked.

"About television," he said.

"Oh, yeah," I squeaked, although I still wasn't completely sure what he meant.

"I hate to say this, but some of the school staff gets here pretty early," Jessica reminded us. "I wouldn't waste time."

No sooner were the words out of her mouth than the doorknob on the lab door began to turn!

38

I caught my breath. Everyone exchanged panicked looks. Had someone discovered us? Were they going to take me away and slice me into little slivers in the name of science?

The lab door opened . . . and Josh and Andy came in.

Whew!

"What are you guys doing here?" Jessica asked.

"We were just wondering if maybe Jake and Howard the alien didn't have to switch after all," Andy said.

"What do you mean?" I asked.

"Maybe we could leave things the way they are for a while," Josh explained. "Like Jake could stay in Howard's body and go back to Howard's planet with Howard's parents and Howard could stay here in Jake's body."

"Then maybe in about a year Jake could come back again and we'll see if you guys still want to switch," Andy said.

"Are you for real?" I asked.

"You might really like it, Jake," Josh said. "That way you can watch all the TV you want."

"And we can hang out with Howard and learn big words to impress our friends and relatives," added Andy.

"Forget it," I said. "I want my body back."

"Then you'd better hurry," Jessica warned us. "We're running out of time."

I went over to the DITS and sat down on one side of the computer console. Howard the alien sat down on the other side. Mr. Dirksen stood at the console. Melvin and Doris held hands and waited nervously.

"I think I should warn you that I've never done this in front of a crowd before," Mr. Dirksen said as he fiddled with some dials. "Sometimes the DITS doesn't work exactly the way it's supposed to."

"Uh, excuse me for saying this," I squeaked, "but as far as I know, it's *never* worked the way it's supposed to."

"Yes, yes, I suppose you're right about that," Mr. Dirksen replied. "Anyway, here goes!"

He pressed the red button.

Whump!

39

When the haze cleared, I was back in my old body!

"Oh, man!" I exclaimed joyfully as I wiggled my fingers. "It's good to be back!"

But Jessica, Andy, and Josh stared at me with amazed looks and didn't say a word.

"What is it?" I asked. "What's wrong?"

"*Ahhhh!*" Doris the alien let out a shriek as she and her husband bent over their son. But they were blocking my view and I couldn't see what was wrong. I turned back to my sister and friends.

"Come on, guys, tell me what happened."

My friends and sister shared a look.

"What do you think?" Josh asked.

"Well, it *is* different," said Jessica.

"Maybe he could use them as goober launchers," Andy said with a grin.

Goober launchers? I reached up and felt my

face. My mouth felt normal. So did my eyes. But when I got to my nose . . .

It wasn't there!

Instead, I still had those two stubby nose tubes.

I quickly looked back at Howard. Instead of having tubes between his beak and his frog eyes, he had my nose!

"That looks terrible!" Doris the alien cried.

"Don't listen to her, Jake," Andy said excitedly. "You have to do something for me. Try to blow out real hard through those tubes. I want to see if anything shoots out."

"Don't do it!" Jessica gasped. "If you think I want to have a brother who walks around the house launching goobers, you're nuts." She turned to Mr. Dirksen. "You have to fix this."

40

Mr. Dirksen turned back to the computer console and adjusted the dials again.

He pressed the red button.

Whump!

The first thing I did when the haze cleared was feel my nose. I had it back again!

Over in the other seat Howard was looking down at his body with a sad expression.

"Oh, Howard, baby, is that really you?" Doris asked.

"I regret to acknowledge that it is," he squeaked.

His mom stretched her long arms around him. "Way cool! It's dynamite to have you back again!"

"Uh-oh!" Jessica pointed out the window. "A car just pulled into the school parking lot. People are getting out."

"Come on," Melvin squeaked. "We'd better go."

"Where?" Mr. Dirksen asked.

"I'll show you," squeaked Howard.

His parents got on their scooter chairs and we all went out the back doors and headed across the athletic fields toward the woods behind the school.

For the first time in days, the sun was out.

"What a bummer!" Melvin complained, shielding his eyes from the sun's rays with his mitten-hand. "How can you stand it?"

"Actually, it feels good," squeaked Doris.

Leading the way, Howard also used his mitten-hand to block the sunlight from his froggy eyes.

"So, uh, listen, Mr. and Mrs. Alien," Andy said as we walked. "In your travels through space, have you ever come across any giant aliens with really big nostrils? Big enough to produce huge petrified goobers?"

Melvin scowled at him. "Get a life, kid."

We followed Howard into the woods, where he led us to two large glass capsules that looked like giant, clear Christmas lights.

"Way cool!" Andy grunted.

"This is what you came here in?" I asked.

"Yes," Howard answered.

"Excuse me for saying this," said Mr. Dirksen. "But these don't look capable of interplanetary travel. There's no breathing apparatus or steering. There's no heat shield for entering the atmosphere."

Howard glanced at his parents. "Mother, Father, you go ahead. I want to talk to my friends for a moment."

Melvin and Doris hesitated.

"You're not gonna pull a fast one, are you?" Melvin asked his son.

"No, Father," Howard replied. "You have my word that I'll come back."

"I believe him," Doris squeaked. "He knows that things are going to be different from now on."

We watched as Melvin and Doris slowly climbed off their scooter chairs and got into one of the glass capsules. Inside they waved at us.

We waved back.

The glass capsule began to vibrate.

Then, right before our eyes, it slowly disappeared.

41

"**H**ow in the world . . . ?" Mr. Dirksen gasped. "Electromagnetic wave transference coupled with turbo lightspeed amplification," Howard said.

"That explains the strange radio signals the astronomers picked up last week," Mr. Dirksen said.

"Yes." Howard nodded. "But the rest of the technology will remain a mystery to your scientists for thousands of years."

"How do you know?" I asked.

"Because I not only come from another planet," Howard explained, "I come from the future as well." He pointed his mitten-hand at the remaining glass capsule. "This isn't just a space vehicle. It's also a time machine."

"You come from the future?" Jessica repeated in disbelief.

"Of course!" Mr. Dirksen cried. "It would take

thousands of years for our television signals to reach another planet."

"But why did you come back through time to see us?" Jessica asked.

"Because I knew you'd still be interesting," Howard replied. "Ten thousand years from now you may be like the people on my planet — lazy creatures with weak legs who hardly ever budge from the television."

"Does that mean Earth will turn into an ugly gray planet, too?" Jessica asked.

"It's possible," Howard replied.

"No way!" Josh refused to believe him.

"It doesn't happen overnight," Howard said. "It's a gradual process. But think about this. Only two hundred years ago, there were no malls, no tall buildings, no cars, no paved roads."

"There were no TVs or telephones," Jessica added.

"People didn't even have electricity," said Mr. Dirksen.

"No video games," said Andy.

"You're right," Josh said. "If the world could change that much in the past two hundred years, just think how much it may change in the next *ten thousand* years."

"I don't like it," Jessica said.

"Maybe it doesn't *have* to happen," squeaked Howard. "Maybe you can stop it."

"How?" Andy asked.

"I don't know," Howard said. "But that is also part of the reason I came here. Not just to enjoy you, but to warn you."

From across the athletic fields came the faint sound of school bells ringing.

"Uh-oh, school's starting," Josh said.

Howard started to climb into the capsule.

"Hey, man," Andy said. "I just want you to know that you may be ug . . . er, *interesting* on the outside, but you're really beautiful on the inside."

The rest of us nodded in agreement.

"I'll miss all of you," Howard said.

"And we'll miss you." Jessica sniffed and rubbed a tear from her eye.

Inside the glass capsule, Howard gave us one last wave.

We all waved back.

The capsule began to vibrate. Then, slowly, it vanished.

42

We stood there silently staring at the spot where the glass capsule had been.

"Hard to believe," Josh muttered.

"He was a nice guy," said Andy.

"Electromagnetic wave transference coupled with turbo lightspeed amplification," Mr. Dirksen mumbled to himself.

"You can't tell anyone," said Jessica.

"Why not?" Mr. Dirksen asked.

"They won't believe you," I said.

"But if we *all* tell them," Mr. Dirksen said.

The rest of us shook our heads.

"We have no proof," said Josh.

"I don't want to spend the rest of my life in the nuthouse," Andy said.

"Me neither," I agreed.

In the distance the second bell rang.

"Guess we'd better go," said Andy.

We all turned and started out of the woods.

"I guess the important thing now is not to forget what Howard taught us," my sister said. "We really should appreciate the beauty of the world around us."

"And not spend so much time vegging out in front of the TV," said Josh.

"I totally agree," I said.

Jessica gave me a skeptical look. "Do you agree enough to get rid of that giant-screen TV?"

"Well, not *that* much," I said.

My sister nodded knowingly. "I figured. Anyway, I'd better get over to the high school. See you later, guys."

We waved good-bye to Jessica and continued into the middle school. Inside, Josh and Andy went to their homerooms. I went into the science lab with Mr. Dirksen.

"Well, Jake," my teacher said. "Being in an alien's body must have been quite an experience for you. Perhaps you'd like to do your report on it."

That reminded me of something. I reached into my pocket and took out the report Howard had done for me.

"Already did it, Mr. Dirksen," I said, handing it to him. "My report on the possibility of life on other planets."

Mr. Dirksen read through the report and started to frown. " 'Our first documented contact with extraterrestrial beings will occur on June fifth, in the year two thousand two hundred and seven, when we will receive a series of coded light signals from a source near the star Alpha Centauri.' "

Mr. Dirksen lowered the report. "I can't accept this, Jake. It talks about events that happen in the future. It's obvious you didn't write it."

"Did, too," I said, holding up my hands. "With these very fingers."

Mr. Dirksen realized what I meant and laughed. "Oh, all right, Jake. On second thought, I'll accept it."

All right!

About the Author

Todd Strasser has written many award-winning novels for young and teenage readers. Among his best-known books are *Help! I'm Trapped in Obedience School* and *Abe Lincoln for Class President!* His most recent project for Scholastic was *Camp Run-a-Muck,* a series about a summer camp where anything can happen.

Todd speaks frequently at schools about the craft of writing and conducts writing workshops for young people. He and his family live outside New York City with their yellow Labrador retriever, Mac.

You can find out more about Todd and his books at http://www.ToddStrasser.com